WINTER OF THE HUNGRY

By Tiffany Kleiman

North Charleston  South Carolina

WINTER OF THE HUNGRY

This is a work of fiction. Names, characters, places, and incidents either are the product of the author's imagination or are used fictitiously, and any resemblance to actual persons living or dead, business establishments, events, or locales is entirely coincidental or have been used with permission.

CreateSpace
4900 LaCross Road
North Charleston, SC 29406
USA

ISBN-13: 978-1537680323
ISBN-10: 1537680323

Printed in the United States of America

WINTER OF THE HUNGRY

In Dedication:
To my husband Jerry ... The one person who has always stuck by me and given me the courage to pursue my dreams, no matter how crazy they may have seemed at the time ... I love you.
To Ann W. for always being my red ink and one of the best editors, and to Ann O. for again tackling the details, layouts, and margins; it is much appreciated.
And to all my past HelpDesk associates for their imaginations.

In Memory of
Jake "Shorts" Dominick
And
Nicholas Pender

~ Gone from this earth too soon ...
... But will never be forgotten ~

PROLOGUE

WINTER OF THE HUNGRY

Reporter: "Here we are, interviewing Gunther Sullivan, the last surviving member of the unbelievable attack on the little island of Marksburg, Michigan. You have lost all your friends, family members, and neighbors to, what the investigators are describing as a horrible accident at a nearby Government testing site, and the incident is under investigation. Can we get your recall of the events?"

Gunther: "Call me Itchy."

Reporter: "Okay, Itchy, how'd you get a nickname like that?"

Itchy: "Josh, one of my friends, well ... he used to be my friend ... well, he put itching power in my jock strap at school before football practice one day and when we were out on the field, I just couldn't stop scratching. Everyone was laughing and the name just stuck. Plus, it's way better than Gunther ... sorry, Mom."

Reporter: "I bet you miss her, don't you?"

Itchy: "Ya (sniff) ..."

Reporter: "Would you like a tissue?"

Itchy: "Ya, I must have come down with a cold. Guess it was from all that running around outside in this snow, heh."

WINTER OF THE HUNGRY

Reporter: "Why don't you tell us what happened, in your own words."

Itchy: "Well, I was playing Xbox with my friend Josh ...

"AAAARRRGGGHHH!"

"Sshh! They'll hear you!"

"Oh, baw! I don't care if your parents hear me or not.

What the hell are they gonna do to me? Kick me outside? It's

fricken' 10 degrees out there and it's the middle of December!

Like I'd freeze or something, geez!"

> *"My idiot friend Josh was always griping. He said it was because he had no parents and was raised in foster care, so he had a right to gripe. He was emancipated at 17 so he could 'get out of the dump', as he would say. He was a tall, lanky, shaggy looking character and had been my best friend for years. His foster home was in my school district and that's how I met him. Yeah, I called him an idiot, but only because I loved the guy ... but totally not in a gay way. Not that there's anything wrong with that or anything! Um, anyway ..."*

"Dude! You know I'm supposed to be grounded and Ma

WINTER OF THE HUNGRY

said no video games, so keep it down or I'm gonna end up outside on my ear!"

"Okay, okay! God! You're starting to sound like me, heh heh heh."

"God forbid THAT happens."

Then I heard footsteps. "Josh! Turn off the damn machine and put the controller back before she sees!"

"Do you kids want something to eat?"

"Sure, Mrs. S." answered Josh.

"It'll be ready in about 20 minutes."

"'K, Mom. Josh and I are gonna go outside and play on the ice; call us when it's ready."

"Don't get too close to the other side of the cove, Gunny."

"Ya, I know, Mom, that's where the thin ice is," I said as I rolled my eyes.

In Josh's best motherly voice, "Oh, Gunny, you be careful now."

WINTER OF THE HUNGRY

"Shut up, Josh!"

"Gosh, don't they know you hate that name?"

"Yes! I've told them a thousand times, but they refuse to call me Itchy, said it sounded like I had some medical issue."

"Well, we all know that you have a medical issue. Hahahaha!"

"Shut up, Josh!"

"That's when the whole house started shaking ..."

"Get into the cellar!" yelled my dad, who was in his study.

I remember my mom screaming and time moved pretty fast from there on. My mom, dad, and I dove into the cellar but not before we noticed Josh wasn't with us and was standing at the window...

"Cool!"

"Josh, get your ass in the cellar!"

"Okay, Mr. S."

"As we sat in the cellar we listened as the whole house shook and we could hear stuff falling off the walls and crashing on the floor. Mom was more worried about Nana's Ming vase than

anything else and was chanting to herself..."

"Please, not Mom's Ming vase; please, not Mom's Ming vase ... "

> *"I overheard my dad once, and I don't know if he was joking or not, but he had said that Nana was cremated and was in the Ming vase and that's why Mom was so weird about it. I always hated that vase after that, creeped me out. So anyway, we stayed down there for about a half hour, not that the house shook that long or nothing but my dad, being from California, was telling us to wait because of aftershocks. I'm thinking this is Michigan, we don't even have earthquakes, but he wouldn't listen to me, like usual."*

"I'll go up and look and make sure that it's safe. You guys stay here."

> *"My dad, always the brave one. That was the last time I saw my dad ... alive."*

WINTER OF THE HUNGRY

CHAPTER 1

WINTER OF THE HUNGRY

"I wonder what's taking Dad so long? It's been like 20 minutes or something."

"He should have been back by now to let us know if it's safe or not. You kids stay here and I'm going to go look. And I mean it too! Stay here!"

"Ya, Mom."

"God, she's so bossy!"

"Shut up, Josh!" I yelled as I punched him. We got into a little punching match, and that's when we heard a blood curdling scream coming from upstairs. It was my mom, and it sounded like something you would hear coming from a horror movie ... little did Josh and I know we were about to be part of one ...

"MOM?!?" I yelled running from the basement, with Josh on my heels. We both ran up the stairs and I yelled again ... "MOM?!? WHERE ARE YOU?!?!" The next thing we saw was something I will remember forever ... my mom was bleeding and had what looked like a bite mark on her arm, and she was crying

WINTER OF THE HUNGRY

hysterically. "MOM! What happened?" I ran around the kitchen grabbing towels and whatever I could find to bandage up her arm and sent Josh to the bathroom to get the first aid stuff.

"(Sniff, sniff, sob) ... I came up here ... (sniff) ... and was looking around for your father ... (sob) ... he ... he ... he was outside, just standing there in the snow ... I said his name as I grabbed his shoulder and he ... he ... turned around and BIT ME on the arm! I screamed and pushed him off of me and ran back inside and locked the door. Your father's eyes ... it's like ... like ... like they were dead ... there was no life in them ... (sob) ... He growled at me like some animal! ... (Sob ... sob) ..."

At that moment I heard this noise that was like a cross between a wild animal and something in horrible pain, and it was right outside the kitchen door. I got up to look and my mom yelled ... "NO! It's your father! Don't let him in!"

"Mom, I just wanna see what that is; you don't know that it's Dad, and why would Dad bite you?" I pulled back the kitchen

WINTER OF THE HUNGRY

door's curtain and saw what could only be explained by believing

in every horror movie you've ever seen ... what I saw was my dad

... and he was a zombie ...

> *Reporter: "Wait! You mean you're telling us that your dad was an actual zombie?! Like a real, live zombie?!"*

> *Itchy: "The government tried to say that it was some kind of chemical spill from the testing site and all the people got sick and died, but that's only part of it. The people in my town DID get sick and die, they just didn't stay dead for long. (Sniff) ... could I have another Kleenex please?"*

> *Reporter: "Sure. I just find it so hard to believe that something from the movies could actually come to life. Go on with your story Itchy."*

... I pulled back the curtain and saw my dad, the zombie. I

didn't know whether to scream or put the curtain back or run or

what. I was the definition of scared. His eyes were crazy.

Nothing like what you see in the movies. It's like they were just

there, with no purpose, like they had no soul behind them. They

didn't look like any contact lens I've ever seen. I just stood there

staring at him as he growled and groaned on the other side of the door, trying to get in. Josh is the one that snapped me back to reality.

"HOLY SHIT! What the hell happened to Mr. S?"

"Gunny, close the curtain! I can't stand to look at him anymore ... (sob) ... I think my arm is going numb."

"Josh, you get the first aid kit? Mom needs it."

"Yea ... Yeah. Is this seriously happening? I mean really? Seriously?"

"I think so, Josh. This is not looking good, Mom; what am I supposed to do?"

"I don't feel so good, honey. Can you get me a glass of water, Josh?"

"Sure, Mrs. S.," Josh said as he handed me the first aid kit.

"Mom, you need to lay down, you don't look so good." I was worried about her as I bandaged her arm, although I didn't know if I was doing it right.

As Josh came back with the water, "'Cause your mom's

turning into a zombie; of course she don't look good."

"Knock it off, Josh! Mom, let's get you upstairs to lie down and then we'll figure out what the hell is wrong with Dad." I led Mom upstairs while Josh followed with the glass of water and followed Mom and me into her bedroom. "Just lie down, okay, Mom?"

"Yes, dear. Josh, where's that water?"

"Right here, Mrs. S." Josh put down the water on the bed stand and helped me pull the covers over my mom and walked out with me as I pulled the door closed.

"Do you really believe this is happening, Josh?"

"If your mom turns, then ya, I do."

"Oh, I don't have time for you and your stupid comments. I gotta find my dad." I ran down the stairs with Josh and into the kitchen. Looking around at all the bloody towels, it seemed unreal that just this morning the four of us were having breakfast together at the stupid crooked island that my dad built in the middle of the kitchen, sitting on old captain's chairs that were made by my grandfather and laughing about how Dad's coffee was slightly slanted because of the crooked island.

I looked outside the kitchen door's window, but Dad was gone. I put my ear against the door, and I didn't hear anything. I was about to open the door when Josh grabbed my hand.

"Are you stupid? You have to get a sharp weapon to jab into his brain in case he's out there and tries to eat you."

"Josh, I swear ..."

"No! I'm serious! Haven't you ever paid attention to ANY zombie movie? You have to stab them in the head in order for them to die. Be smart! The stupid ones are always the first ones to get eaten in a zombie movie!"

"I'm not gonna stab my dad in the head! And I'm not stupid!" But just to make sure, I went to the living room and grabbed a fire poker from the fireplace stand. I mean, Josh was right. Anyone that's seen a zombie movie knows you have to have

WINTER OF THE HUNGRY

a sharp weapon; I just wasn't sure I could actually use it on my dad, zombie or not.

I looked up and saw all our family pictures sitting on the rock mantel that my dad had personally put together just because my mom asked him too. The mantel was made with all the rocks from around the yard or from the woods behind the house. There were gray, red, and black rocks and in a random pattern from the floor to the middle of the wall. Dad shaped them all together to fit just right and made it for my mother for their 25th anniversary. Took him almost four months to finish it, but it must have been perfect because my mother cried. At least it was a lot better than the kitchen island.

Looking at their wedding photo, which was black and white, and in it my dad was dipping my mother, I thought to myself there were no two people that loved each other more than them. I sighed, as I put the picture back on the mantel and turned around to find Josh staring at me.

WINTER OF THE HUNGRY

"What?"

"Nothing. I'm just glad that I'm here and not out there somewhere alone. You guys are my family," Josh said as he walked over to the mantel and grabbed the picture of all four of us from the day we went to The Mall of America for a weekend. "I just can't image having to deal with something like this alone."

"I'm glad that you're here too, Josh," I said as I took the picture from him and wished my mom would come downstairs and hug me like she was in the picture. She always made me feel safe, and right now that was one feeling that I didn't have. I set the picture back on the mantel and looked at Josh, "I guess we better go find my dad."

We walked back into the kitchen and checked the window in the kitchen door and didn't see my dad. I listened to see if I could hear him outside, and there was no sound. So, one look at Josh, and I opened the door slowly. Now, I forgot the kitchen door squeaks, and when I started to open it, it let out this nails on the

Winter of the Hungry

chalkboard screech, which made both Josh and me jump.

Normally we open it fast to avoid the noise, but this time there was

a reason for taking my time. The screech, however, apparently got

my dad's attention, wherever he was hiding at, and he came

barreling through the door with a ghastly growl and drool hanging

from his bottom lip. Josh and I screamed, trying to push the door

closed and shove my dad back outside, but even with the both of us

pushing, for some reason, my dad was stronger than he ever was

before.

"Let go of the door and get out of the way!" I yelled at

Josh. He stepped back at the same time I did, and Dad crashed

through the door and the weight of him pushing made him fall on

the floor. I jumped on top of his back and yelled at him, "Dad!

Dad!" I got no response but groans and he kept trying to grab my

legs or arms or anything within his reach to bite me.

"I don't wanna do it, Dad, I don't! Don't make me do it!"

"Fine, I will!" Josh grabbed the fire poker out of my hand

and jabbed it through my dad's head. Dad stopped moving and I sat there on my dad's back for what seemed like ages, trying to process what just happened in front of me. Looking down at his green flannel shirt and remembering I had gotten it for him for his birthday this year. He wore it so often that Mom practically yanked it off of him once so she could wash it. I got off my dad and, with a deep breath, pulled the fire poker out of his head. With a tear escaping my eye, I rolled him over. What I saw didn't look a thing like my dad. His eyes were blank, his face looked like no human face should look. It was even more distorted than it had been before, distorted and just wrong; it was all wrong. I didn't hear Josh shut the kitchen door and lock it behind me, but I did hear the thud from upstairs. I turned around and looked at Josh, and I knew ... my mom.

I looked at my dad one last time as Josh and I ran up the stairs to my mom's room. There were the same groans and noises coming from behind the door as my dad had been making.

WINTER OF THE HUNGRY

Looking at each other, Josh and I knew this was real and what had to be done.

"Let me do it, Josh. She's my mom."

"Will you be able to?"

"Dad, I didn't believe; I believe now. I can do this, I have to." But in the back of my head, I was scared. Scared to death. Did I really have enough guts to stab my mother through the head with a fire poker? Are zombies real? God, I hope I'm dreaming. I looked at Josh, "Are you ready?"

"Hafta be, don't I?"

"Okay, on the count of 3, open the door. 1 ... 2 ..."

"WAIT! Are we going on 3 or 3 then open the door?"

"On 3, we'll go on 3! Geez, Josh!"

I tried listening to see exactly where the sounds were coming from inside the room, and it sounded as if whatever it was was away from the door so I looked at Josh, "Are you ready now? We go on 3." Josh nodded. "1 ... 2 ... 3!" Josh whipped open the

Winter of the Hungry

door and the sight that stood before me was no longer my mother.

Her eyes were bloodshot, and the bite mark on her arm was a

gruesome black color, the same color as her nails on the opposite

hand, as it looked as if she pulled the bandages off to scratch it

while she was still Mom. Half of the bandages were still hanging

from her arm.

She ran at us like a rabid animal when she saw us standing

in the doorway, and I yelled, "Mom, don't. Please don't!" I raised

my arms and lifted the fire poker eyeball high ...

CHAPTER 2

WINTER OF THE HUNGRY

"We have to get out of here, Itchy. We can't stay in this house. Gotta get off the island to the mainland. Where's the keys to your dad's boat?"

"We can't leave yet. I have to bury my parents. I'm not gonna leave them lying on the floor, especially Mom. Plus, I wanna clean up that mess."

"Ya, I can't believe that. She flew."

"JOSH! Really? That's my mom you're talking about."

"Sorry ... Sorry, Mrs. S.," he said, looking at her smashed body under the balcony. Mom hit the fire poker but was running with such force that she went about half way through the fire poker before I let go and stepped to the side as she went barreling over the railing, falling to the floor. She hit the marble so hard it bent the fire poker around her head. "Guess we need a new weapon," stated Josh. Always Mr. Obvious. I'm just glad she didn't feel anything ... I hope.

I got the cleaning supplies from the hall closet and the

WINTER OF THE HUNGRY

bucket and filled it with hot water from the tub when we heard

screams. "What the hell was that?" Josh asked, rushing into the

bathroom.

"I don't know. Maybe someone's in trouble." We ran out

of the bathroom and into the front hallway and looked out the front

door to see our neighbor, Toni, running from what looked like her

boyfriend Jasper. Toni was tall and semi-pretty, physically fit with

dark brown almost black hair. Jasper was a muscle freak body

builder, looked like he had no neck, and had arms full of tattoos.

Toni and Jasper were an on again off again couple that were

always fighting about something. Jasper really was a jerk, though,

so I don't know why Toni stayed with him. However, she couldn't

pour water out of a boot with instructions on the heel, so maybe

Jasper was the only one who could stand her. I don't know, but I

opened the door anyway. "Toni! Come over here! Hurry!"

Jasper heard and saw us but continued to follow Toni as she started

running toward the front door, and right when she got to the sidewalk, she tripped. Jasper was on her like a cougar pouncing on a meal and started devouring her piece by piece. She screamed, and the sound that came out of her mouth was like someone who was drowning and spitting out water but in this case it was blood. Then as soon as it began, she was dead. I heard Josh throw up, and I thought I was gonna be sick, but Jasper heard the noise Josh had made and his head snapped up. With blood and guts and gore hanging from his mouth, in one sharp move, he jumped up and ran straight toward us. I slammed the door and hit the deadbolt right before he hit the other side and started growling and scratching to get in like a rabid dog.

"Can I kill Jasper?" asked Josh.

I actually laughed. "Why?"

"He threw a rock at my head once and told me there were no hoboes allowed on his street. I hate the fucking guy."

"I guess we gotta get used to it. Gonna hafta kill Toni too. If this is like any movie we've seen, she'll turn now that she's been

WINTER OF THE HUNGRY

bitten ... er ... well ... eaten."

"I don't think you are going to have time to clean up this mess and bury your parents, Dude. Seems like the longer we stay here, the more zombies show up. We have to get off the island."

"I think we need to figure out what the hell happened first." I looked around the room and thought to myself, what should we do? "Um ... okay ... find something to kill Jasper with and try to call someone, Toni ain't going anywhere for the moment; I'm gonna turn the TV on and see if anything is being reported."

"Yes, Sir!" Josh said as the smart aleck saluted me and turned military style towards the kitchen. I walked around my mother and into the living room to turn the TV on. At first I couldn't get my fingers to hit the right button on the remote to turn the darn thing on and I realized I was shaking. Well, of course I was shaking! I had just watched my best friend kill my father, I stabbed my mother and watched her volley over the railing to the floor, and I just saw my neighbor's boyfriend kill her with his bare

WINTER OF THE HUNGRY

hands and teeth.

Taking a deep breath, I finally hit the power button. The TV clicked on with a loud crash and boom because the volume was up past 60 since we had been watching a movie last night and the DVD player's volume is too low. I hit the volume button and tried turning it down, but I was too late. Jasper came crashing through the living room window and would have probably gotten me, because I fell over in the chair and knocked it over halfway on top of myself, but he got caught in the gold tassels hanging down from the red satin curtain my mom just had to have and struggling around, got all tied up.

Josh came running in the room with an axe he later told me he found in the basement and swung it at Jasper's neck, or at least where it should have been. It's totally not like the movies. The axe got stuck not even a quarter of the way in and that pretty much just pissed Jasper off. He started attempting even more to get loose and at the same time trying to bite Josh. Josh was struggling to get the axe loose so he could swing again, but the gold tassel frayed and Jasper got loose. I ran for the fire place and grabbed the fire tongs and jumped over the overturned chair and pinched Jasper's neck with the tongs. It wasn't very tight because of the axe but it held Jasper still long enough for Josh to pull out the axe and rear back.

"Ready, 1 ... 2 ... 3 ... let go!" Josh said as he swung the axe again, this time with all his might. In that same instant I relaxed the fire tongs and pulled them away to give him free rein over Jasper's neck. This time it went a little more than half way through, enough to knock Jasper off his feet, but still not enough to keep him from moving. Josh pulled back and swung again, this time sending Jasper's head rolling across Mom's Persian living room rug, adding all sorts of new designs to the already wild pattern.

"GREAT! Now we really can't stay here. The stupid living room window's broken!"

WINTER OF THE HUNGRY

"Keep your voice down, Josh," I barely breathed as I sat down on the floor to catch what breath I had left. "We don't know how many more are out there." I grabbed the remote and started flipping through channels, but all the channels had blank screens and said 'No Signal'. "Guess we better try the radio in the car," I shrugged. "Anything on the phone?"

"No, nothing but 'Not in service, please try again later'," Josh mimicked in the annoying operator tone.

I got up off of the floor, and Josh and I grabbed everything in the house that we could carry to either protect ourselves or feed ourselves. My dad was a gun nut, so it wasn't that hard to go into the game room and break open the gun cabinet and grab those. Plus, he had tons of protective gear left over from his days as a K9 trainer for the Marksburg PD. Granted, most of the stuff we were carrying was pretty heavy, and wearing the suits didn't help, but we didn't want those zombie creeps biting us. At least I knew they wouldn't be able to bite through these suits. The kind of suits my dad had weren't the big bulky ones that you see in movies either. These were competition suits and were made for agility and speed, so we didn't look like a bunch of colorful sumo wrestlers waddling down the street unable to outrun these undead things.

"Josh, we gotta give them a name."

"Huh? Who?"

"The zombies. We gotta call them something."

"How about ... zombies?" He responded, making a face.

"No. I mean in every movie or TV show they call them something. If they ever make a movie about what happened here I wanna be the one that comes up with the name. I'd go down in history!" I chuckled.

"Whatever. I don't know ... Daisy Pushers," Josh laughed

"I'm serious, think, Josh." As I finished putting on my armored motorcycle boots ... well my dad's boots, but I don't think he'll be using them anytime soon. "How about the Extinct?"

"Naw. The Mortified." Josh nodded and smiled at me.

Winter of the Hungry

"The Carnivores?"

"Ah crap. It's snowing again," Josh stated as he looked out the sliding doors. "Maybe all the dead will freeze in the snow and then we can just walk around and shoot them all in the head."

"That's it, Josh! You're a genius!"

"I am? Why? What did I say?"

"You said the dead walking around in the snow! The Snow-Bies! That's what we'll call them."

"I still like The Mortified better," Josh pouted.

"Oh, shut up and help me find the keys to the car." I thought to myself that maybe we did need a better name for them, but it would have to wait until later.

We both headed back into the front of the house, and I went to look at the front door where Mom usually hangs them if she uses the car last. Josh headed into the kitchen to see if they were hanging by that door. I had a bad feeling they were in my dad's pockets, and I didn't want to go through them to look. I sighed as I

WINTER OF THE HUNGRY

walked into the kitchen to join Josh and bent down beside my dad to see if either pocket had the keys. Yup. Right pocket, just like always.

Now came the hard part. We had to walk from the front door across the lawn to the garage. I always told my dad we should have connected the garage so we didn't have to walk outside to get to it, but I guess it's a little late to be upset about it now. Josh and I looked around the house one last time and then looked at each other.

"I guess the adventure begins," Josh shrugged.

I opened the front door slowly - this one didn't squeak - and looked around outside. Nothing, except Toni, who had come to and was growling around on the ground and starting to move towards us since we had opened the door. She was a little slow since one of her legs was about bitten off, so I wasn't worried; all she could do was drag herself with her hands. I shut the door behind me and, out of habit, made sure it was locked. I gave Josh the key to the car and walked toward Toni. She was still crawling on the ground towards us. When I walked up, she reached out for me, making sucking noises and other ones I couldn't describe since Jasper had bit out her throat. I stood there staring at her for a few seconds.

"I never really liked you anyway," I said as I stomped on her head with my boot until there was nothing left but brain matter and hair. Then I turned and walked toward the garage with Josh.

CHAPTER 3

WINTER OF THE HUNGRY

Sebastian's severed head went rolling across the floor. Josh was getting pretty good at that, especially since he had sharpened the blade in my dad's garage before we left. We had taken my dad's car and driven through the town and saw only the occasional person wandering around scared or already dead. We did see a few people that were stuck in vehicles because of a car accident or whatever had happened, but we didn't dare get out of the car or stop. We've seen the movies; that's usually when the zombie you didn't see jumps out to eat you while you're helping the innocent person in the car. Granted, we wanted to help, but it was just too risky and dumb.

There was nothing but static on the radio, so we decided to stop by a few friends' houses to see if anyone was still alive, which is where we found Sebastian. He was our first stop. Even though this idea was a little dumb too, we just couldn't pass up seeing if our friends were okay. Strangers were one thing, but friends? We weren't that heartless.

WINTER OF THE HUNGRY

Sebastian was this little Irish dude that used to help me with my homework. He was a pretty smart kid. He was on the chess team and the debate team, and when the computers all crashed in the school, instead of calling in the professionals, our principal called Sebastian. He had it up and running within about an hour.

He had this sister that was, well, a babe! Everyone at school loved her. She was taller than Sebastian with red hair like his but longer and the greenest eyes you could ever imagine. Even her name was beautiful ... Scarlett ... (sigh). Too bad she's dead now.

We drove up to the house and slowly got out of the car and listened for any noises or sounds of life. Nothing close by. Walking up to the door, Josh asked, "Should we go in the front? Maybe we should sneak around back?"

"Why? You think zombies would knock and someone on the other side is gonna shoot the door? Get real, Josh!" We

WINTER OF THE HUNGRY

decided to knock and see if anyone answered, hoping nobody shot through the door.

"Go away!" said a sad voice on the other side of the door.

"Scarlett?" I asked.

"Itchy?" We heard footsteps and then the door unlocking. The door slowly opened and the beautiful creature I had come to love to look at was covered in blood, her makeup running down her face and her hair matted. She looked like she had just been in a car accident.

"What happened to you? Are you okay?" I asked as she leapt into my arms. "Come on, let's get off the porch and inside before we are seen. Josh, close and lock the door." Scarlett let go and walked to a chair in the center of the room. The living room was a disaster, and there was blood everywhere. The chair she was sitting on was facing the doorway that led into the dining room, and next to her chair was a Remington 11-87 Sportsman Synthetic Semi Auto Shotgun. I got to know guns because of my dad, so I was pretty good at spotting and being able to name them when I see them. Plus, I knew what kind of gun Scarlett's dad hunted with because he used to go waterfowl hunting with my dad. She picked up the shotgun and put it in her lap.

Josh went to look around, and I knelt down next to her. "Are you okay?" I looked over at Josh and told him not to go far till we knew what happened.

Scarlett started telling us her story. "We were all outside, just enjoying the nice day in the snow. Dad was shoveling the driveway, and Mom was cleaning off the porch. Sebastian and I were just horsing around and throwing snowballs and building snowmen and stuff. I wasn't paying attention and Sebastian snuck up behind me and got me in the back of the head with a snowball and it fell all down my back ...

"You asshole! Now I gotta go inside, dry off, and change!" Scarlett swore as she stomped into the house.

"Sorry, Sis," Sebastian apologized, between laughing

snorts. He sat down at the counter and was doodling on some notepaper trying to think of something he could get her with on her way back down the stairs. After a few minutes, Scarlett started coming down to put her boots back on and go back outside when there was this loud bang. "What the hell was that?" Scarlett barely heard Sebastian before she lost her balance coming down the stairs and then hit her head on the wall.

He went running over to his sister to see if she was okay and ran up to get the first aid kit from the bathroom when he happened to look out the window in the upstairs hallway and saw this cloud of purple haze drifting over the island coming from the government facility that was at the edge of the island. He also saw his mom and dad down in the front yard; they were hugging each other and looking at the purple haze too, along with a lot of the neighbors, and then they all fell on the ground and started having seizures. Sebastian ran to the phone and called 911 but the phone was busy. "How the hell could 911 be busy?" he said, slamming

WINTER OF THE HUNGRY

the phone down.

Sebastian ran back past the window on his way to the stairs and saw all of them get back up off of the ground and watched in horror as some of the neighbors' family members had come out to check on them, and they attacked the ones that had been in the house and started eating them! The purple haze was gone, and he was so scared because he knew what was going on, being the horror nut that he is. He ran past Scarlett on the stairs and ran straight into the basement and locked the door. All he could hear from the outside were moans and screams but after a while he heard Scarlett call for their mother. "She's alive ... oh no, she doesn't know! I gotta stop her from opening that door!" Sebastian said to himself as he ran for the basement door to unlock it.

"Mom? Mom?" Scarlett mumbled as she started to wake up. "Where the hell is everyone? How long was I out?" Touching her head to see if the pain radiating from her temple was bleeding, she heard moans coming from outside. "Oh no, they're hurt."

WINTER OF THE HUNGRY

Running outside Scarlett saw her mom and dad just standing there, "Mom, Dad, are you guys okay?" That's when they turned and started running for her. Sebastian pulled Scarlett back inside and tried slamming the door before their parents got there but he couldn't, and the weight was too much for him to keep them from pushing inside.

Scarlett had no clue what was going on but there was a huge knife on the table that Sebastian apparently had prior to pulling her inside, which he grabbed and started slicing up his parents. "Aaaaaaaaahhhhhhhhh!" screamed Scarlet which attracted the attention of her mother who turned and started towards her. She was bleeding from all the cuts from Sebastian and looking nothing like Scarlett's Mom. Scarlett ended up backing herself into the corner by the stairs and was frozen with fear. She didn't know what to do, and her mom was trying to bite her, snapping her jaws at each lunge forward. All she could do was cry and keep pushing her mom away, "Mom, stop, please stop!", but then she just stopped moving. Sebastian had poked the knife he had grabbed through the top of their mother's head, then it disappeared again as he pulled it out, and their mother fell with a thud to the floor.

Sebastian stood there covered in blood with the knife, and their dad was on the floor by the front door. Sebastian walked over to the front door, closed and locked it. "Sit down," he said to Scarlett as he walked over to her.

When Scarlett finished her story, "I just can't fathom it, real live zombies. Oops, what an oxymoron, zombies take over the world and I forget proper grammar," she said, sighing. Scarlett looked at us like we had some answers for her on why this was happening. I actually started to wonder where Sebastian was now.

"So ... where is Seby?" asked Josh, using Sebastian's nickname that he gave him back in first grade.

"He's upstairs in his room, he said he wasn't feeling well after we put Mom and Dad in their room, so he said he was going to lie down for a bit, and I was to stand guard. He pretty much said the world was turning into the undead, and we had to survive. I didn't have a doubt in my head that he was anything but right. So, I went and got Dad's hunting gun and pulled the chair toward the stairs because if Sebastian wasn't feeling well, I knew it was only a matter of time before he turned, and I was in no way in Hell gonna be eaten by my snot nosed little brother."

"How long ago was that?" I asked, trying to remember how long it took Mom to turn.

"I don't know, I really haven't been watching the time."

I looked up at Josh and nodded upstairs. "Go upstairs and listen and see what's going on. Don't open the door though." I turned back to Scarlett, "Are you okay? Were you hurt or anything?"

"No, it's all blood from Mom and carrying her and Dad to their room. I just wish I was brave enough to take a shower and clean up; I'd probably feel better if I could do that."

WINTER OF THE HUNGRY

"Well, let's see what's going on with your brother, and then we'll go from there, okay?"

"'K."

At that point Josh came down, "No sounds coming from the room but heavy breathing. He could be sleeping," he said, as he shrugged his shoulders.

"We have to go and check; Scarlett you stay, here. If by chance he is a zombie and he gets by us, you gonna be able to shoot him?"

"Pretty sure; aim for the head, right?"

"Ya. We'll be right back. Be ready."

Josh and I headed upstairs and walked to Sebastian's door. "Do you think he turned?"

"I don't know, Itchy. I hope not. I kind of liked the little fart. Besides, he's smart; we could use him to figure out what to do about the mess we are in."

"Sounds like he's been hiding more than he's been

thinking, Josh, but we'll cross our fingers just in case." I listened against the door and déjà vu came because of the situation with my mom, but I didn't hear moans or any other weird sounds coming from the room except for heavy breathing like Josh said. "I guess we should just open the door and get it over with."

"On 3?"

"On 3, 1 ... 2 ... 3!"

Josh whipped open the door and all we saw was a sleeping Sebastian snap awake and yell, "What the Hell, guys!"

"We thought you were a zombie, Seby," Josh joked.

"Well, I'm not, you dork, but you almost gave me a heart attack! Where's Scarlett? Is she okay?"

"She's fine, she's downstairs," I told him.

That's when Scarlett came running in. "Sebastian! You're okay!? I heard the voices downstairs and knew you weren't a zombie!" giving him a big hug.

"Wow! Thanks, guys. It makes me feel all warm and

WINTER OF THE HUNGRY

fuzzy that my two best friends AND my sister all thought I was dead and walking around. No faith, geesh!"

"Well, it's cause you said you didn't feel well before you went and laid down. I thought maybe you got bit or scratched or something and you didn't tell me," Scarlett explained. "So, I told the guys that and they were gonna, ya know, take care of you if you were ... ah ... dead."

"Oh, well, in that case, thanks, guys. REALLY?! Wow, I'm glad I woke up or I'd be headless right now. Nice axe, Josh." Rolling his eyes.

"How do you expect us to act, Seby? Do you have any idea what me and Itchy have been through?"

"Do you have any idea what Scarlett and I have been through? I just needed a nap and of course I didn't feel well; I had to kill my parents. Made me sick to my stomach."

"So, now what?" asked Scarlett.

"Pack more supplies and hit the road, I guess. Josh and I

WINTER OF THE HUNGRY

are heading towards my dad's boat 'cause there's no phone reception, no signal on the TV, and nothing on the radio. I think we're on our own here. We were just gonna stop at as many people's houses that we knew to see if they were still alive and then head to the mainland."

"Well, guess Scarlett and I will pack up what we can here and ride with you guys?" Sebastian asked.

"Ya, I guess. If we pick up more people, we'll have to get another vehicle then." I thought to myself as we left the room and started looking for stuff that Sebastian didn't look so well. He looked sick, like sweaty and stuff, but at the time, I wasn't thinking clearly. I should have paid more attention.

"You got all the food, Scarlett?" Josh asked as he walked into the kitchen. "I don't think you're gonna need that though," Josh laughed as he called for me. "Itchy! You gotta come see this!" More laughter.

"What's going on with you two?" I asked coming from the

WINTER OF THE HUNGRY

pantry. And that's when I saw that Scarlett was trying to fit this

big cake into a bag, and Josh was standing there laughing at her.

"What are you doing?"

"Mom made it, it was supposed to be my birthday cake,"

Scarlett replied with sad eyes. I forgot it was gonna be her

birthday tomorrow. Damn, how could I forget that? She looked a

lot better since she showered and changed clothes, but those eyes

still looked so sad it could break your heart.

"With all that's been happening, I forgot, Scarlett, I'm

sorry. How about we have a piece now and sing 'Happy

Birthday'?" I asked grabbing some plates from the cupboard.

"I s'pose," she replied, moping. "Where's Sebastian?"

"Ya, where is Seby?" asked Josh.

"Sebastian!? Get your butt out here and help us sing

'Happy Birthday' to your sister!" I yelled as I found some candles

in the drawer and was lighting them with matches I found in the

same place. We started singing, figuring Sebastian would join us

WINTER OF THE HUNGRY

in a second.

"Happy Birthday to you, Happy Birthday to you ..."

Scarlett screamed ... "Sebastian!"

Josh and I whirled around to see Sebastian; he must have gotten scratched during the fight with his parents, and while the rest of us were looking for supplies, he had died and turned. Our friend was now a zombie. "Josh! Grab the axe!"

Josh had set the axe on the table next to the counter and reach out for it the same time Sebastian started running for us. "Sorry, Seby!" Josh said as he swung.

CHAPTER 4

WINTER OF THE HUNGRY

"Damn, that cake looked really good too," whined Josh once the three of us were in the car.

"Shut up, Josh! Really? How can you think about cake?" I asked looking at him angrily.

"'Cause I'm hungry?"

I guess I was too and hadn't really thought about it because of all the events today. I remembered we were about to have lunch when the bomb, or purple haze, or whatever happened happened, and this once happy day turned into a nightmare. "Guess we better eat something." I had Scarlett reach into one of the bags and grab some apples and crackers and cheese that I had grabbed from my house and hand them to me and Josh. She had been pretty silent since we left the house and started driving down the road. "You doing okay, Scarlett?"

"I don't know, I guess. I lost my whole family today, didn't get to celebrate my birthday, and the really sad part? It might be my last day on Earth, and I have to spend it with you and

Josh."

Ya, she was gonna be okay, I thought to myself, as Josh and I giggled at her. Josh was still trying to find something on the radio, but it was still nothing but static.

"Quit playing with the knobs, Josh! You're gonna break 'em!"

"We gotta see if there's anything on any of the channels. How we gonna do that if it sits on one station and we don't touch it?"

"Well, give a rest a while then." I wasn't really watching the road and that's when we hit something. I slammed on the brakes, and Scarlett hit her head on my shoulder.

"Ouch! Geez, Itchy! Where'd you get your license? Out of a Cracker-Jack box?"

"From Mr. Mayfib, just like you did." I said as I looked around to see what we hit. That's when I saw someone getting up off of the street behind our car. "Shit! I hit someone." I grabbed the door handle to get out and Josh grabbed me.

"What are you doing? Don't get out, we don't know if they're dead or not."

We all looked behind the car and saw what was left of whoever I had hit lumber towards us. She couldn't move very fast because of whatever had tried to eat her, and plus, I'm assuming, me hitting her with the car.

"Do you know her, Itchy?" Scarlett asked

"I don't think so. But it's really hard to tell considering how she looks; she did fly pretty far from the car."

"Well, let's not wait till she gets closer, let's get out of here," Josh screeched. I turned to find out why. There were zombies coming out from all corners of the houses. They must have heard the tires squeal when I hit the brakes, and they were coming right for us. I threw the car in drive and found that the tires were just spinning and making just as much noise peeling out of there right as one of the zombies reached the back bumper of the car, before it caught traction and leapt forward. Scarlett screamed.

"At least we know we can't stop like that and we need to be quiet when we are outside. One noise, and they come running," Scarlett said with a little shake.

"Either that or Itchy has to pay better attention to the road," Josh complained. I just stuck my tongue out at him.

We decided to take a ride by the radio station to see if anyone was still in there. The radio station was a small building in the center of the island that was run by Mark, who's known as our local leper, because he's missing an arm. At least that's what he tells people, that he came from a leper colony on some distant island where body parts just fall off of people and he happened to lose his arm before he left there and came to our little island. I actually heard once though that his arm was shot off in Desert Storm trying to save a friend; the friend didn't survive. Sad story; I guess that's why he tells people the other one.

He also had this insane obsession with the color yellow.

WINTER OF THE HUNGRY

Everything he owned was yellow; house, clothes, hair, a yellow tabby cat, even his car was yellow, a yellow 1974 AMC Gremlin, with a hideous red stripe down the sides. He said yellow made everything bright, and we needed more brightness in our world. Which is also why he became a DJ, so he could bring happy music to people's lives.

As we pulled up to the station, I noticed that all the curtains were closed, which is unusual for Mark because of his bright cheery attitude. Said we should always let the sunshine in. "I wonder if he's in there?"

"His car is here," Josh pointed out.

"Well, let's go look. If he is, maybe he heard something on the radio before it went off the air," Scarlett hoped.

The radio station was in an open area on top of a hill; we could see all around it and saw no zombies, so we all got out of the car and headed for the door. Josh and I listened and heard nothing.

"Maybe we should knock first like we did at Scarlett's?"

WINTER OF THE HUNGRY

Josh suggested.

I reached up my hand to knock and Scarlett had been looking around as we stood there, "The curtain moved! Someone's in there!"

I knocked and the door whipped open and there stood Mark in all his yellow dress but he was full of blood, and for the first time since I've known him, he wasn't smiling. "Get in here! Quick!" he said, as he shoved us all inside and looked back and forth out the door before shutting it and locking it. When he turned around, I noticed he was holding a chef's knife in his hand. "Are any of you bit? Tell the truth!" he said looking at the three of us like he'd lost his mind.

"No, none of us are bit, Mark," I answered.

"Show me!" he yelled, then put his head down and looked at the closed curtains like he was gonna wake someone up with how loud he was. We all put our arms out and turned around like criminals being searched. "Okay, okay ... (sigh)," as he slid down

WINTER OF THE HUNGRY

the wall to sit on the floor.

"Mark, are you okay? Where'd all the blood come from?"
I was curious. Nobody else is usually up here and there were no
other vehicles outside, so I couldn't figure out why he was full of
blood.

"It was Larz, that crazy hippy. He came up to get some
water from the tap outside, which he usually does and came in to
say hi and warm up before walking back to his cabin back in the
woods. We chatted for a bit about the government and how it
sucks and yadda yadda, normal complaining shit, and then he left.
Wasn't two minutes and the whole station shook and that ceiling
tile fell on me and knocked me out," he said, pointing up to over
where he usually sits.

We all looked to see the hole in the ceiling where the tile
should be and down to the broken pieces on the floor under it.
"One of the boys from the edge of the lake, um ... Deryk, I think
his name is, was here using the bathroom 'cause he was walking

WINTER OF THE HUNGRY

back from a buddy's house and decided to go through the property. I had completely forgot he was here till that bomb or whatever it was went off and I woke up to him shaking me asking what the heck happened."

Mark stopped to put the knife down and wipe his face. He was sweating, not from being warm, because it was cold as hell in the station, but I think 'cause of nervousness. He eyes kept moving like he was waiting for something to happen. "I asked if he was okay while I rubbed my head, cursing at the tile that fell on me, and then the both of us went outside to see what happened. Figured something blew at the government place. We were standing outside when I thought I heard a weird noise, like an animal or something, but I wasn't sure 'cause the whole time the station was still playing the afternoon Christmas music. I heard it again and this time I was sure I heard it, and turned around to see Larz heading towards us like he was hurt and gone mental or something. Deryk went running over to help and that's when Larz

WINTER OF THE HUNGRY

bit him. I ran over and grabbed Deryk and punched Larz in the face, and he didn't even flinch.

"I pushed Deryk into the station and was yelling at Larz to get out of here before I called the cops and that's when he lunged at me, knocking me over, and tried taking a bite out of me! Deryk had seen my lettuce knife, grabbed it and stabbed Larz in the head. He instantly stopped moving. I shoved him off of me and got up to help Deryk who had fallen against the wall. He was pretty badly shaken up and was bleeding pretty bad too. Larz took a huge chunk out of his shoulder. I'm surprised he didn't collapse sooner. Had to be the adrenaline."

"I ran to the bathroom to get rags or whatever I had here to help him, but by the time I got back to him, he had lost too much blood I guess, and had died." Mark started crying. "He was only a boy, what was he? 15-16? I don't even know. I stared at him for a while and decided to call the cops and tell them what happened, but the line was dead. Figured whatever that boom was had taken out a wire somewhere. So, I shut the radio off and made an announcement that the radio would go off the air but would report anything it hears as it comes. Figured Larz heard the music and that's why he came back this way."

"As soon as I shut the music off I heard that weird sound again and turned around to see Deryk getting up off of the floor! I mean how could he? He was dead! He started toward me and I was like, shit! The knife was still in Larz's head, and Deryk had that same look in his eye that Larz had. I ran to Larz's body, pulled out the knife as Deryk attempted to attack me, and I put the knife up as I slipped on Larz's blood and ended up on my back as Deryk jumped on top of me and the knife went into his mouth. Totally gross. I pushed him off of me and got up. Fucking zombies? Really?" Mark shouted, as he got up off of the floor and danced around the room in a fit of rage like he was stomping on bugs.

"Where are they now, Mark?" Josh wondered.

WINTER OF THE HUNGRY

"I took them out back to get them out of my station."

"You just threw them outside? Like garbage?" Scarlett said, shocked.

"What would you have liked me to do with them? Leave them laying by each other in front of the door? Geez! I wanted to clean up the mess and I didn't know how long I was gonna be in here and I wasn't going to be in here with two dead bodies that came back to life once already and smelling them rot."

"How they gonna rot in this cold ass station?" whined Josh.

"Gotta conserve on heat, dude. So, what are all of you up to? Why did you come here? I mean, I'm thankful that you did, but why?"

"We wanted to see if you were still here and if you had heard anything about what the hell is going on here? The TV is out, the radio was static and none of the phones are working. Figured maybe you'd have some info if you were still here," I explained.

WINTER OF THE HUNGRY

"Naw, haven't heard a peep. I mean I got the old walkie-talkies, but I didn't even think about that until just now. Let me see ... where did I put them?"

As Mark went to find the walkie-talkies, Scarlett sat down in one of the chairs, and Josh and I looked around for any supplies that we could use along the way. Figured we'd have Mark take his car and follow us to the boat launch; we were running out of room in my dad's car.

"Good thing I kept these old things, hey?" Mark said as he came back with the walkies. He had kept them as a reminder of his friend that passed away. They were the AN/PRC-148 Multiband Inter/Intra Team Radio or MBITR walkies, and the only reason I know that is because it was written on the side.

"Cool thing about these babies is that they are encrypted so nobody can listen in," Mark said smiling.

"Good. Those snow-bies might listen in and then they'd know where we are," Josh piped up rolling his eyes.

WINTER OF THE HUNGRY

"Snow-bies?" Mark asked.

"Ya, some stupid name that Itchy came up with."

Mark turned the walkies on and made sure they worked and that's when we heard, what Mark referred to as 'chatter'. It sounded like an old war movie to me, but Mark's almost plastered smile faded.

"Shhhhkkkk ... 10-4 we are flying overhead now, looks like a cluster fuck down there. People killing people all over the place."

We looked out the window and saw two jets flying over us. "Those are U2-Dragon Ladies," Mark told us.

"What kind of jets are they?" asked Scarlett.

"Reconnaissance aircrafts, kind of like spies; they look at stuff and then relay back to headquarters what they see."

"Shhhhkkkkk ... It doesn't look good. I'll do another pass over and head back to base."

"Roger that, Blue-20."

WINTER OF THE HUNGRY

Mark opened the door and went running outside; we followed him and started waving at the jet as it flew over us. "Shhhhhkkkk ... base we got some people waving and jumping on a hill by a small building, should I request a rescue pickup?"

"Negative Blue-20, we can't risk it. We don't know if those people have been exposed or not. Continue your aerial search and return to base."

"10-4."

"What the hell?" shouted Mark. "They can't just leave us on the island, those bastards!" flipping off the sky.

"What do they mean exposed? Exposed to what? What do we have?" cried Scarlett.

"They just don't know what's going on down here and think that everyone here was exposed to whatever that purple haze was that Sebastian saw. Calm down, Scarlett, we'll just get to the lake and explain to them what happened. Seems that anyone that was inside at the time of the explosion is okay, anyone that was outside turned into a zombie," I said as I hugged Scarlett.

"Let's just get the rest of the stuff and get the hell out of here. That jet gave me the creeps now," Josh said as he walked back in the station.

"Is that the plan?" asked Mark. "We're going to be going to the lake and then what? I doubt they are running the ferry right now if they won't even land a plane."

"I have my dad's boat," I answered.

"Well, I'm gonna go get some of my other toys from the good ole' days," Mark winked as he walked back into the station while Scarlett and I followed, and then he took off into the back room. We were loading everything into the car when Mark came out of the back room with tons of army stuff. "Now we are ready for those zombies! I got M67's, M84's, MK 1's, and my favorites, Molotov Cocktails!"

"What the Hell, Mark? You keep those in the radio station? We aren't going to war," Josh laughed.

WINTER OF THE HUNGRY

"Yes, we are! The Snow-bie War! You can never be too careful anyway. I'd rather be safe than sorry." I knew Mark was right, and somehow didn't want to believe that those things might actually be the only way to get off this island, and that's even if the Government soldiers on the other side would let us.

We all piled into the two cars. Josh decided to ride with Mark, and Scarlett and I rode in my dad's car. We took off down the hill and headed back towards town. By this time it was getting later in the evening and we found that while we were away from the town so long, a lot of the people that had been alive no longer were, and they were all over the place.

"Shit! How are we gonna get through town?" Josh voiced over the walkie.

"I don't know, plus, we still got to stop and see if Ramsey and Duff are still alive," I answered back.

"Damn! I forgot about that."

"And Aaron!" chimed in Scarlett grabbing the walkie from

me.

"Awww, fu ..." Josh and Mark's walkie cut off. I snickered because I knew why. Josh hates Aaron.

Aaron was the high school quarterback, so describing him was like something right out of an 80's movie; broad shoulders, tall, blond hair, Mr. Popularity, and totally in love with himself. Pretty much, he was a jerk, and he was Scarlett's boyfriend. So, of course, I didn't like the guy much either. He thought he was tough, he didn't do any of his own homework, and he flirted with all the girls when Scarlett wasn't around. Makes me want to punch him, but I never did. Should have, but never did.

Josh's voice came over the walkie, "Do we have to go by that jerk's house?"

CHAPTER 5

WINTER OF THE HUNGRY

Ramsey and Duff were the couple of the year. Always together, always happy, always sickening everyone out with how much they loved each other. Ramsey was average height, with glasses, and short brown hair, and a little round, but not fat. Duff is tall, skinny, and has long blond hair and a perfect face with a little mole on her cheek. She kind of reminded me of an actress with perfect features and a smile with high cheekbones. So sexy. If they had survived this horrendous ordeal, then they'd be together in their favorite meeting place ... the basement of the school. So, after we got to the "Jerk's" house, as Josh would say, the school would be our next stop. Which, with any zombie move ever made, you know was the last place you would want to go, even if it was Christmas vacation. It's the first place all the kids go because it's the only place that they feel safe besides at home.

Turning onto Rosemont Street where Aaron lived, we all noticed that there were no zombies anywhere. But there were cars all over, some on fire, along with one of the houses. Scarlett screamed; one of the houses on fire was Aaron's house. We cautiously got out of the vehicles and looked around; seemed the zombies weren't too keen on fire and left this section of neighborhood for one that wasn't so hot.

"I hope he's not in there!" cried Scarlett.

"Shhhhhh ... we don't see any zombies, but that doesn't mean you have to call them all back over here with your loud screeching!" yelled Josh.

"Well, what do you suggest we do?" asked Mark, as everyone else looked at me.

"Why are you all looking at me? I didn't ask to be in charge!"

"No, but you're the one running around rescuing people, and Josh is a moron, so you're the only feasible option as a leader," Mark retorted.

"Hey!" Josh frowned as he flipped Mark off.

"Well, then I guess we'll look around and see who or what

we can find, but be careful everyone; Scarlett, stay with me." I

hated being in charge; nobody ever listened to me, but for some

reason, everyone seemed to be a little calmer having some kind of

orders to follow. Scarlett and I went up to Aaron's house to see if

we could get close enough to look inside and see anything. It was

completely engulfed, but would have been a total loss anyway,

even if the fire department was still operational. Speaking of that,

"I wonder why we haven't seen any police or ambulances or fire

trucks anywhere?"

"Ya, that is weird," Scarlett agreed. "Maybe they never

made it out of the center of town? People trying to head to the

boat launches probably jammed the roadways, and they couldn't

get through to help anyone ... oh God! That means there's nobody

out there to help us! And we have to go through the center of town

to get to the boat! We're never gonna make it!"

"Snap out of it, Scarlett!" I said, as I shook her and slapped

her across the face. "Calm down, this is not the time to start

WINTER OF THE HUNGRY

freaking out! We have to stay together so we can get through this." That's when Scarlett screamed.

Pointing behind me, the basement door of Aaron's house popped open and this wet blanket started coming out from inside. I was getting ready to attack or run, depending, but Scarlett's scream attracted our friends and a couple of other lingering nearby zombies that were within earshot, that Josh and Mark quickly took care of. Her scream also alerted whatever was coming out of Aaron's basement, and it turned out to be Aaron under the water soaked blanket to escape the fire.

Throwing the blanket off of himself, he came dashing over to Scarlett, "Whoa, babe. You okay? Oh, I'm so glad to see you are not one of them. I knew my baby could survive. Thanks, doofus, for bringing my baby to safety," He said smugly, as he glanced in my direction.

"Ya, whatever. Let's just get out of here before we attract all the zombies in the neighborhood." Walking back to the car,

WINTER OF THE HUNGRY

"Why in the hell did you light your house on fire anyway, Aaron?"

"Well ... I was in the basement working on my pectorals,"
he began as he bounced each muscle like some bodybuilder, "and I
was listening to my jamming music, just in the zone, man, ya
know? I almost lost my grip on the weight bar when the house
shook, and was like what the fuck?"

"Ma, hey, Ma? What the heck was that? You blow up the
stove?" chuckling to himself. There was no answer from upstairs.
So, going upstairs to find his mother, he found she had gone
outside to look at the purple plume of smoke that had appeared
over the island.

Through the open kitchen door she called to Aaron,
"Aaron, you gotta come look at this!"

"Naw, I'm going back to work out. Who cares about some
stupid cloud?" he answered as he walked back to the basement
door and closed it behind him. He walked down the stairs, not
knowing that this was the last time he'd ever see his mother alive.

WINTER OF THE HUNGRY

Turning his music back on and lying back down on the weight bench, he began to lift his weights, thinking to himself that he eventually wanted to be able to lift 275 pounds and was proud that he was able to lift 230 pounds at the moment. That's when he heard the banging on the door to the basement.

"What the hell?" Aaron said turning off his music, listening.

"BANG, BANG, BANG!" came the noise from the door.

"Ma, is that you?" Aaron asked as he got up from the bench and started up the stairs.

BANG, BANG BANG!"

"What the Hell, Ma?" He reached for the door and, opening it, found his mother standing there, and she jumped at him as soon as the door was open, toppling both of them down the stairs. On the way down something cracked; it was his mother's ankle.

Getting up off of the floor, Aaron backed away from his

mother, "What the fuck, Mom? You trying to kill me?"

Because of her ankle, she wasn't able to stand and run at him like the hunger wanted her to, and she had to lumber forward, limping. Looking down, Aaron saw that there was a piece of bone sticking out of her ankle, but looking back up, it looked like she didn't even notice.

"Mom, what's wrong with you?" A groan of mindless hunger was all he got as a reply. "Seriously?" Aaron asked no one in particular as he turned and ran up the stairs. He was looking around trying to figure out what to do, when their neighbor, Mr. Troy, who was always hitting on his mom, came stumbling in the open kitchen door that was never closed. Mr. Troy however, gave Aaron the conclusion on what exactly was going on, because Mr. Troy was missing half his bottom jaw and he was full of blood. "Shit!" Aaron yelled as he ran to the cabinet to find the knives, but Mr. Troy was on him before he could get to one. "Mother fucker, get off of me, you stinky undead bastard!" He shoved Mr. Troy

WINTER OF THE HUNGRY

off of him and started to get up when he realized his mother had made it all the way up the stairs with her broken ankle and was right in his way at the door. He grabbed the rolling pin off the table, which his mother had been using to make pies before the explosion, and bashed Mr. Troy in the head, knocking him into his mother. He then ran around the counter and noticed there were more undead neighbors starting to cluster towards the kitchen door, being attracted by all the noise and yelling. Aaron still couldn't get near the door but ran upstairs to the living room and grabbed the lighter fluid that was next to the fire place. Basically, it was there because Aaron was lazy when it came to lighting the logs and didn't feel like sitting there with kindling and waiting. He then grabbed the grill lighter off the mantel and started squirting the lighter fluid everywhere. "Let's see how you shortsighted mindless moronic flesh eaters like being on fire." Aaron lit the lighter fluid and watched as it followed the trail back to the mantel as his zombie neighbors and mother were heading up the stairs towards him. He ran down the back staircase and turned back towards the kitchen to come up behind them and leave another trail to block them coming back down, but he couldn't get back to the front stairway due to the undead in the kitchen so he just squirted them instead, and set them ablaze.

Aaron turned down the basement steps and grabbed a blanket out of the laundry basket by the washing machine and doused it in water from the basement sink. Looking around he actually felt sad that he had burned up his childhood home, but it was to protect himself against the horde that had invited themselves in. Thinking of his mother, he couldn't help but feel that he was actually doing her a favor, so she could die in the house she called home and not out on the street somewhere. He covered himself up as fire and pieces of flooring started falling from the ceiling above and ran to the outside access doors of the basement to the outside.

"And that's when I came out the doors and found you

guys." Aaron turned to look at his home which was totally engulfed in flames as the group walked back to the car and noticed the blaze was actually attracting some zombies that were nearby.

"Aaron, we got to get going," Scarlett said, tugging on his arm.

"Ya, I know." Looking back at the house one last time, "Bye, Mom. I love you."

Piling into the cars, Josh radioed to me, "Where we heading now?"

"To the school; we got to go find Ramsey and Duff." I answered, throwing the car into gear and taking off, swerving around some of the zombies meandering in the street, while Mark and the others followed in his car.

CHAPTER 6

WINTER OF THE HUNGRY

Meanwhile across town ...

Ann thought to herself that she couldn't believe this was happening. She was just dumbfounded as to what was actually going on. Zombies? She was scared to death. She would have been hysterical if it wouldn't have been for Jay. That was one thing she was happy to say was also unbelievable ... he had come back for her.

Over the last nine years that they had been together, Ann and Jay never had what you would call a perfect relationship and after they were married it only got worse. Finally, they decided it was time for a divorce. Although they loved each other more than life itself, they just had too many problems; whether it was money, trust or lack-there-of, insecurities, and never seeing eye to eye; they both were just tired of arguing, and it was time to call it quits.

Ann had divorce papers drawn up that morning and Jay had already moved out a few days before. She had been up in her room crying when she heard the boom and sat up from her bed to

WINTER OF THE HUNGRY

look out the window to see the purple haze sweeping over the town. She was in awe, and the first person she thought of to call to tell about what she was seeing was Jay. This just made her lie back down and start crying again.

She must have cried herself to sleep when she heard the banging and woke up. Ann ran down the stairs to the door and looked through the peep hole; it was Jay. Opening the door, "What are you doing here?" she asked, trying to hide the overwhelming joy she felt at seeing his face. Jay wasn't what you would call star quality but Ann found him handsome. He had a round face and a bald head; even though Ann preferred longer hair on men, she didn't mind that Jay was bald, except for his thick brown mustache. He was taller than Ann, but to her, everyone was taller, so she was used to it. Ann was only five foot two and had short straight sandy blond hair that curved around her face. She was a little on the heavier side and wished she had the motivation to lose some weight, but she just liked chocolate too much.

WINTER OF THE HUNGRY

"Haven't you seen what's been going on out here?" Jay asked, as he looked over his shoulder at her while closing and locking the door behind him.

"No. I had fallen asleep. Why? What's going on?"

"You are not gonna believe this, but there was an explosion earlier ..."

Ann interrupted, "Oh, ya. I heard that. I looked out the window and saw these purple clouds or whatever and I thought about calling you but ..." She trailed off noticing that Jay had blood on him. "Jay, you're bleeding!"

"No, it's not my blood. That's what I was trying to tell you, the purple dust stuff made people act like they were having seizures and I was looking out the window drinking coffee when I saw it. Neighbors that had been outside just falling and flailing their arms all over the place and then they all just quit moving. I had dropped my coffee and was getting my boots and coat on and was about to open the door when I heard the screams. I opened the door and saw neighbors attacking their families that had come out to help them. They were acting like zombies!"

"You're pulling my leg Jay, right? Zombies? I don't believe you."

"As serious as I'm standing here. I ran back in the house and grabbed my pistol and knew somehow, some way, I had to get to you. I'd never be able to live with myself if something had happened to you. Divorce or no, I love you, and I had to see if you were okay.

"Oh, Jay!" Ann cried as she hugged him, stopping the hug as quickly as it started because of all the tension due to the divorce. "But," looking at him, "what about the blood? You said it wasn't yours? Whose is it?"

"Remember Mrs. Windimere?

"The widow with all the cats?"

"Ya. She must have been outside and when I left the house she came tearassing across the street like there was no tomorrow.

WINTER OF THE HUNGRY

I've never seen an old lady move so fast. So before she got close enough to bite me, I shot her. Guess some of the blood must have sprayed on me. That's when I got into my truck and drove here."

"Oh, Jay. What are we going to do? Where will we go? Should we stay here?"

"I don't think so, my love. We need to get off the island. It won't be long before this whole place is overrun with zombies."

"What if this is everywhere and not just here?"

"I guess we'll just have to take that chance. Let's pack up some stuff."

Ann couldn't help but wonder, "How did some purple cloud make everyone have seizures and turn into zombies? I mean, really, this isn't some movie. Stuff like that just doesn't happen ... does it?"

Stopping what he was doing, Jay turned and looked at her. "Well, I guess it doesn't really matter if I say anything now," he said, sitting down.

Winter of the Hungry

"What do you mean? Jay? What do you know?"

Jay works security at the Government testing site, and he has clearance to pretty much all the areas in the compound. "You hear things, ya know? Working in a place like that. But we are not just sworn but contracted into secrecy. If I would have said anything or if anyone finds out I did say anything, if we get out of this, they pretty much have permission to erase me."

"To kill you? Are you kidding me?"

"People go," holding up two fingers on each hand making the quote sign, "''Missing' all the time. All these," finger quoting again, "'accidents' that you hear about on the news with some important person involved? They are not really accidents. Take Mr. Blackstone for instance."

"Seriously? Mr. Blackstone? I thought he had a heart attack and crashed his car?"

"No, I had seen him the day of the accident and he had been fighting with General Garaff about some sort of ethical issue.

Winter of the Hungry

It was something that Mr. Blackstone, didn't like and actually told the General he wasn't going to keep quiet about it and then stormed out of his office. Later that day he was dead. I don't think that was just a coincidence."

"He's the nicest old man I could have ever known. What the hell could have been so important to keep quiet that Mr. Blackstone deserved to be killed? They could have arrested him or done something other than kill him." Ann sat down next to Jay on the bed and sniffed. "That's just not right. I can't believe this is happening, it's so surreal."

Jay put his arm around her. It was the first time he had touched her, besides a couple of hugs here and there, and an overwhelming feeling of love came over him. Ann felt the touch and nestled into his shoulder. As he pulled her closer, he whispered, "I love you, and I'm not going to let anyone or anything hurt you."

"I love you, too." She looked up at him and, leaning

WINTER OF THE HUNGRY

forward, kissed him for the first time in weeks. She felt her heart skip a beat and every muscle tensed up, the heat started to radiate between them.

He touched her ever so slightly on the hip, picking her up and setting her up farther on the bed. Lying down next to her, he looked into her eyes, "I've missed you."

"I've missed you, too." She put her arms around him and pulled him close.

He slowly undressed her, with passion in every touch to her skin, and undressing himself, he crawled in close to her and they made the most magical, poetic, utopian love that they had ever done before.

Eyes glazed over in pure seduction satisfaction, she struggled to focus in on his face, "I don't want a divorce," she said, starting to cry.

Jay held her close, "Neither do I."

After getting redressed, Ann asked, "What were you going

to tell me before that was so secretive? Before you told me about Mr. Blackstone."

Jay sighed sitting on the bed to put his socks and shoes back on, "Well, like I said, working at the facility you hear things, but you keep your mouth shut, ya know? Well, over the last few months I starting hearing about the doctors there working on a project that could cure ailments."

"What kind of ailments?"

"All ailments. Cancer. Aids. The common cold. Everything. They had been working on it for a long time but I only started hearing about it a few months ago because they were testing it on lab rats or what-have-you, and it was working. Only problem was that after the disease the lab rats had was cured, the rats died but still had movement after death. They attributed it to something like muscle spasms, you know?"

"Like the twitching of limbs, like a leg of a spider still moving once it's been pulled from the body?"

WINTER OF THE HUNGRY

"Ya, kind of like that. I don't know exactly how they were moving, like if it was just a limb or something but the doctors were in an uproar over it because even with the side effect the serum or whatever it was, had worked."

"That's one heck of a side effect, honey. There's no way that the FDA would allow something like that on the market if they knew it would kill people after it cured them."

"I know, so I'm thinking that they've been tweaking it since then, trying to modify it so the rats wouldn't die afterwards. Not sure what kind of progress they made because the talking quit in the hallways. Everything became really quiet. Nobody was talking to anybody so there was nothing to overhear anymore. I have no idea what they did with the project after that. I just assumed they scrapped it."

"So, what does that have to do with the purple cloud?"

"I'm thinking they continued working on it and decided to test it on humans but like you said, the FDA would never approve

WINTER OF THE HUNGRY

human experimentation with the known side effects. So, because of the island, and pretty much being cut off from the world, I think they decided to test it on us and see what happened. If something went wrong, they would just blow up the island or something to cover up what they did and start over. I think that's what the purple cloud was: that stuff they had been injecting the rats with, only in some sort of form that it would cover the island and anyone outside at the time would get infected. I wonder, though, if the government knew that their wonder drug could be passed on through DNA? That every time someone is bitten they turn also?"

"Probably. The government had those test rats; they had to have known what would happen."

"I just can't believe, well, I can, that the government would release this terrible stuff on an unsuspecting island knowing what it could do to people, AND knowing it could spread the way it has. I mean, hasn't any of those stupid idiots ever watched a zombie movie? Didn't they know what they had there? It wasn't a cure, it was a goddamn death sentence for this island, and if it ever gets off the island, the world."

"You know, I've never hated living on this island until they built that damn facility. I know it gave a lot of jobs to islanders but still, I always had a conspiracy theory in the back of my mind about something just like this happening to our happy town. I wonder how many people we know are even still alive? I wonder if anyone at the facility itself got infected?"

"Well, being winter there's a lot more people indoors than out, but today had such a beautiful morning that a lot of people went outside. Especially the kids. I saw a few as I was driving here from my mom's."

"That's so sad, those poor kids. By the way, where is your mom? And Joe? You didn't have to ...?"

"No, but I'm afraid we might run into them, they went to the store this morning because we were out of milk," Jay answered thinking of his poor mother and his step-dad at the

WINTER OF THE HUNGRY

grocery store probably scared out of their minds not knowing what was going on or understanding and probably worried about him. As much as he hated to think it, he would much rather them be already dead, than hiding in a corner frightened about what was going on in the world around them. "We have to go down to N&P and find them before anything else."

"Then, we have to go to the school," Ann said as she packed some clothes in a backpack. She was a teacher and knew that if any of her students survived and weren't at home safe with parents or someone else to protect them, they would end up at the school, the only other place they probably would feel safe. "I have to see if any of my students survived. The school is in the center of town, and I'm sure there are going to be survivors there."

"Probably a lot of hurt and zombies too. There's gonna be a lot of protecting and shooting and the possible killing of friends and kids. You gonna be up for that?"

"If I have to bash some poor kid's head in, in order to

protect myself long enough to get off this island and live happily ever after with my husband," she answered, as she turned with the divorce papers that were in the dresser drawer and ripped them into small pieces and threw them in the garbage by the door, "then G.I. Jane I will become." She may be a teacher, she thought to herself, but she wasn't stupid; she knew what had to be done, but being honest with herself, wasn't quite sure when the time came if she actually would be able to hurt a child she knew. She cared about all her students; how do you kill someone you care about?

Jay was thinking the same thing as he and Ann walked down the stairs to pack up what food they could that wouldn't go bad. Granted being in security, there's always that chance that you would have to shoot someone to protect the company that you're working for and the information in it, but this was different. These were people he knew. Mrs. Windimere was just a neighbor and Jay didn't know her all that well, but still he knew who she was. What happens when it's his mom or Joe that he has to shoot?

WINTER OF THE HUNGRY

Would he be able to, even if it was to protect his own life or Ann's? Little did he know, he would find out the answer to that question ...

CHAPTER 7

WINTER OF THE HUNGRY

"Looks like everyone had the same idea we did," said Josh over the walkie.

There were more cars and zombies the closer I and the rest of the group got to the center of town. A lot of them were wandering around the church.

I saw Stacy Hanson clawing at some poor soul lying on the ground with intestines hanging out of her mouth. She was the least religious person and the biggest slut that I knew. I figured that there would have to be a zombie apocalypse and for her to show up at church to atone for her sins. "Fat chance, Stacy," I muttered to myself, snickering.

"What was that?" asked Scarlett.

"Ah, nothing, just seeing people that I know and thinking out loud. Ya know, we need to get out of this crowded area. It's getting too hard to drive through here with all the abandoned cars," I said into the walkie.

Mark came back over, "Yup, looks like we are gonna have

to blast our path the rest of the way to the school. I noticed some of them aren't moving as fast as they were before. Wonder if the longer they are dead, the slower they get?"

"Looks like it, but there are still a few quick ones out there. Better still keep an eye out. Although that is gonna help us get to the docks quicker if they keep slowing down," I answered back.

"If they slow down enough, we could just go around and shoot them all and clean up the island, and then we'd have the place all to ourselves." Mark retorted smiling to himself.

I nodded, "But it's getting dark and we have to find a safe place to sleep. We won't be able to do anything more until it's light out again, at least not safely."

"If we can sleep," Scarlett interrupted.

"Well, let's get out and start walking to the school. We have to get in there before it gets too dark so at least we'd be able to see anything coming at us," I explained.

"Ya, that's a good idea! Let's get going," Josh ordered.

WINTER OF THE HUNGRY

We parked our cars in a less zombie populated area and gathered as much of the stuff as we could carry. "Be sure to be quiet. Not many of them are quick, but I don't want to try to outrun the ones that are," I explained. I just hoped that when we got inside the school there wasn't a ton of zombies in there too. I didn't want to start blasting my way through fellow classmates to get out of there. But I knew I would if I had to; I had to survive for my mother's sake. I could hear her voice in my head now, saying, "You better survive and carry on the Sullivan name, Gunther." I had to do it, for her.

The five of us walked as quietly as possible through the crowd of cars, ducking and sneaking around the zombies. Most of our noise was covered by the other noises of the zombies, or the muffled screams from other areas unseen, or cars running that the owners hadn't had a chance to shut off. We got pretty close to the school doors, but there was no coverage between the last car and the school doors, which were at least twenty feet apart. Any zombie that was looking in the direction at that moment would see us and the surge towards the school doors would begin.

"I'm thinking we have to run two at a time, so the snow-bies don't see us." I advised. "That way they don't look up and see five people run across the parking lot in a line."

"I don't know how safe that is?" questioned Aaron. "I mean, getting us all inside would be the best thing, wouldn't it? That way we all are safe instead of some inside and some outside. What if the snow-bies, or whatever you call them, see the first two and then the last three are stuck out here? Kind of a dumb idea, if you ask me."

"We didn't!" Josh chimed in.

"Ya, but I think Aaron is right. We need to all run and get in those doors as fast as possible." I didn't like the idea because it was more of chance of being seen, but we needed to stick together. Just then I got an idea, "Anyone think that the doors may be locked for the winter break?"

WINTER OF THE HUNGRY

"Oh shit! No!" Josh all but yelled, as he face palmed himself.

"Sshh! You idiot! You're gonna get us killed with your loud mouth!" whisper/screamed Scarlett.

"During the school year when the janitors were gone for the day, they always left the front doors unlocked in case any students forgot homework or whatever. I forgot a lot of homework," Aaron told us, rolling his eyes at himself. "I don't know if it's true during the winter months though."

"I think that's the first almost useful information you may have given us. Thank God you were here to tell us NOTHING!"

"Josh! Knock it off." I was trying to think of what to do when I heard something. It was a new sound than what we had been listening to while we were sitting there debating on how to get into the school.

"Is that a truck?" Scarlett asked.

We all turned around and looked down Mulberry Street and

WINTER OF THE HUNGRY

saw a Government Issue security truck plowing through the middle

of the street with a zombie horde running and scrambling behind

them in tow.

Scarlett was the first to see who was inside the truck,

"That's Mrs. Dreggy with her husband!"

They pulled right up on the front steps of the school and

jumped out of the truck. Scarlett yelled, "Mrs. Dreggy!" Waving

her arms, she got up and started running toward them. We all

followed suit since Scarlett's yells and the zombie horde following

the truck were coming closer; it wasn't safe to just sit there

anymore. Mrs. Dreggy ran up to the school doors, unlocked, and

opened them. It was a good thing she was there to unlock them

because we didn't have a Plan B for them being locked. Mr.

Dreggy was right behind us shooting any snow-bies that got close

enough as we all ran inside and Mr. Dreggy pulled the doors

closed behind us while we all kept pulling on the doors so Mrs.

Dreggy could lock them. One of the snow-bies got their arm in the

WINTER OF THE HUNGRY

door and was snarling and clawing to get all the way through the space in the door. Josh used the axe to hack off the arm and Mrs. Dreggy locked the doors. Snow-bies were banging into the door and clawing at it, Scarlett let out a little muffled wail as she hid her face in Aaron's chest. Looking out through the windows I could see Stacy Hanson clawing against the door with her one remaining arm. Boy, that's got to suck.

"Well, that was close. What the hell were you kids doing out there? You could have been killed running around making noise like that," scolded Mr. Dreggy. "Are any of you bit, or scratched?"

A big unison "No" came from all of us. However, one of us was lying.

"It's a good thing you two showed up, Mrs. Dreggy. We were hoping the school doors were unlocked," I told her.

"They wouldn't be during winter break. Nobody is here to monitor the halls. Janitors are all on vacation too. Principal

WINTER OF THE HUNGRY

Wooley may have been here, and he would have left the doors unlocked while he was here. Let's get away from the doors and find someplace not so creepy and loud."

I never knew Mrs. Dreggy to take charge like that, but it's possible that a situation like this could change a person, and maybe that nice teacher we used to have had a strong side that none of us had ever seen. Well, that's not true. I saw her get into a parent's face once during a PTA meeting that my mom drug me to when Silvia Brownstone's mother blamed Mrs. Dreggy for her daughter's low grades. Mrs. Dreggy stood up from her seat and point blank told Mrs. Brownstone that her daughter needed to hand in her homework and participate in class to earn the points needed to pass, not just be present to waste space. There were kids in different countries that would kill for a chance at an education, and it's not fair that Silvia is abusing that right when others could profit more from that seat. Just being in class does not guarantee an 'A'; effort is what gives the students their grades, no effort, the grades reflect that effort. Mrs. Dreggy had to apologize to Mrs. Brownstone for calling Silvia a waste of space, but everything she said was true. Silvia pretty much just showed up and sat there all class period. If Mrs. Dreggy called on her, she'd moan and say she didn't know and go back to scribbling in her tablet.

Silvia was the emo/goth of our school. She dressed all in black and smoked cigarettes under the bleachers during lunch hour by herself. She never really hung around with anyone, except Lucy. Lucy was the nice person in our school. She said hi to everyone but never really hung out with any specific group of students. She did, however, hang out with Silvia more often than not. We always used to kid that they were lesbian lovers and Silvia was the butch. Lucy really was nice, though. I wonder where they are, or if they are even alive?

Walking into the principal's office, we noticed a cup of coffee on the desk and the coffee maker was on. This meant that Principal Wooley was in the school somewhere, and if he didn't show up to see what all the ruckus was when we first ran inside, that couldn't be good news.

That's all I needed was to have the guy we nick named Wooly Bully, because he was the meanest principal we had ever heard of, kill me and make me a zombie. It would have been the ultimate bully. The last time that I had a run in with Wooly Bully was right before winter break when he came up to me in the hallway and told me I had been suspended and needed to spend the afternoon after school scrubbing gum off of the desks in all the class rooms. I couldn't figure out why and I asked him why, and he said it was because it needed to be done and I was the first kid he saw when he stepped out of his office after he thought of it. I called my dad on lunch that day and told him what happened and he called the school and having dealt with Wooly Bully before, told him that we were leaving on a family vacation and I needed to be home right after school that day. I felt sorry for Dustin, who was the second person Wooly Bully ran into after me that day, and who ended up being the one who had to scrape the gum off all the desks in the classrooms.

Dustin was what the girls called good looking, and he did a little bit of everything, he played tuba in the band, he played on the football and basketball teams, and he always wore dress pants and silk shirts. I think the girls just like rubbing the shirt, 'cause personally, I thought he was a dork. He moved to the school in 7th grade and became the hit of the school, Mr. Popularity overnight, but he also was popular with the teachers, because he was always in trouble. Hit one kid in the hallway for just looking at him funny. Dustin's dad always got him out of trouble though, at least when it came to missing school. When it involved being in school, his dad made him do whatever Wooley Bully said; that's how he got stuck with the gum job.

In fact, "Wasn't Dustin supposed to be clearing out old lockers or something during winter break, Mrs. Dreggy?"

"I believe so, Itchy. They were supposed to get new

Winter of the Hungry

lockers through the winter break, and Mr. Wooley had Dustin

helping to haul them in when they arrived. I thought they were

supposed to arrive this week sometime, but I still see the old ones

are in. Maybe they didn't get delivered yet?"

I thought to myself that I had seen some hauling trucks

outside, but since we ran inside in a panic, I couldn't tell ya what

the trucks said on the side. Just great! Now we have I don't know

how many moving men, Dustin, Wooley Bully, and Ramsey and

Duff wandering around the school. Plus, whoever else had the

idea of coming here for safety. Somehow this place feels like the

least safe place in town.

CHAPTER 8

WINTER OF THE HUNGRY

Simultaneously under the school ...

"I'm so scared."

"Oh, shut up, Tommy!" Grace ordered as she punched Tommy in the arm. "Why do you always have to be such a chicken shit? We've been in the tunnels under the whole town and there have been no zombies the whole time we've been down here. Now, shut up so I can find the damn door to the basement of the school," as she flicked on her lighter.

Tommy whimpered a small, "Okay."

"Ah ha! There it is!" Grace exclaimed as she found the door. There was a loud creak, but the door always did that, because Grace and Tommy were always in the underground pipes. It's how they got past everyone and skipped school without it being noticed that they left. Grace shut the door as Tommy meandered through it. "Now, we just have to get to the lunch room to eat. I'm starving," as she searched around for the pull cord for the light.

WINTER OF THE HUNGRY

"Ya, me too. Wasn't it lucky that we ran into each other after this all started? I don't know what I would have done if I didn't find you."

"I know, what would you ever do without me? Sometimes you are the creepiest person I've ever met. You'd probably even keep me if I turned into a zombie just so you could still have me around, rotting in your bedroom," Grace turned and wiggled her fingers at him, "As all my parts rotted off."

"I would not!" But Tommy thought to himself that she actually said she'd be in his bedroom. Oh, what a thought. Tommy is the epitome of weird and loves all that tech stuff, he's really into RPG's or roleplaying games and sometimes tries to convince Grace to "role play" with him, just not in the same way he would with his buddy Sam. Sam is another RPG-er and he and Tommy would go to all the RPG camps and/or fairs for days at a time and pretend to be anyone they want, because sometimes it's better than who they really are. One time Sam got to be King

WINTER OF THE HUNGRY

Arthur Pendragon and Tommy was his most trusted knight. However, Grace likes the both of them just how they are and thinks all that RPG stuff is stupid. Tommy tells her she just doesn't understand and should try it. She could be his queen and they could play castle. While lost in his thoughts, Tommy wondered where Sam was, or even if he was still alive.

Tommy has had the biggest crush on Grace for ages, but Grace just wants to be friends. He is constantly trying to get Grace to have sex with him as a courtesy, as a way of helping him cope with his love. Grace always thought he was kidding around about being in love with her. "You know we may never get the opportunity to grow old and what a waste it would be if we never even got the chance to have sex with each other. We should take advantage of the fact that we are safe here and enjoy what may be our last moments together," Tommy advised as he leaned in for kiss.

Grace face palmed him and pushed him away laughing,

WINTER OF THE HUNGRY

"Oh my God, Tommy! Is that all you ever think about is your hormones?"

Tommy wished she could see how much he loved her and just wanted her to notice that he was a hell of a lot better than those biker guys she kept trying to go out with. They all treated her like shit, but he, he treated her like a queen. He always was there when she needed someone to talk to and didn't leave her hanging, waiting on the porch for him to show up when they had plans together. Why couldn't she see what was right in front of her face?

Tommy was an average height, average build, average everything type of guy. He had dark brown hair that was kept messy and draped down in his face. He wore flannel shirts over t-shirts which he had a various collection of; ranging from gaming to movies. He always wore jeans, and most of the pairs he owned were all ripped in the knees, and along with the jeans he always wore high-top shoes; black ones with rainbow laces. He had a semi-clear complexion, with the occasional zit here and there, and had one light brown mole on the side of his nose. He hated it, but Grace thought it gave him character.

Grace was pretty much the same, average everything with short blackish hair, piercings in every spot she could fit on both her ears, and wore pretty much the same style of clothes as Tommy except instead of t-shirts she wore tank tops in a slew of colors. She had a leather bracelet that she always wore that had a skull imbedded in the center, and an orange tear drop charm on a black cord that hung around her neck. She preferred being barefoot to wearing shoes, but when she had to wear them, like to go into N&P, the local grocery store, she slipped on her flip flops.

All of a sudden a face appeared from the dark corner of the room that led to the first floor stairs, "Aaarrrgghhhh!" screamed Tommy as Grace kicked whoever it was, not waiting to find out if it was friend or zombie.

"Ooof!" breathed Ramsey, as he blocked the kick from Grace's foot from barely hitting him square in the nuts and then stayed bent over to compose himself for a second. "That was a close one. What the hell, Grace?"

"Ya, what the hell?" came a voice from inside the dark and then Duff stepped into the light of the boiler room.

"Sorry, didn't know you two were down here."

"Well, that's a dumb statement. Where the hell else would we be?" asked Duff as she rolled her eyes.

"You know what I mean. I didn't know you guys would be here NOW. You know? During the zombie apocalypse?"

"Ya, well, we figured it was as safe as a place as any because nobody ever comes down here and we wanted to be safe from those things outside. Hey! Are any of you two hurt, or scratched or whatever?" asked Ramsey as he stood in front of Duff.

Grace answered, annoyed, "No, we're fine, geez. I'm sick of this shit. Is it safe down here or what?"

"Ya, we've been down here for a while. Haven't heard

nothing much, but with the brick we probably wouldn't. Just
wanted quiet after what we went through to get here." Ramsey
looked back at Duff as Duff lowered her head.

"What happened?" asked Tommy.

"I don't wanna talk about it," snapped Duff.

"Let's just say that Duff's Aunt Katie had an accident and
is no longer with us," whispered Ramsey.

That's when Duff lost it. "An accident? Seriously? She
was hit by a fucking car as she tried to run across the street to help
out Mr. Moothe! I just stood there and watched as Mr. Moothe ran
over to her and just started chewing on her leg!" She sobbed. "If
it wasn't for Ramsey driving up and grabbing me, I would have
been next on Mr. Moothe's list of snacks!" She turned her head
into Ramsey's chest and cried.

"Wow, sorry, Duff," Grace sympathized, thinking of what
had happened to get her and Tommy here. Grace didn't show a
soft side often, but when she watched her brother Zach turn and

start eating her cat Spike, she actually felt sad. Not so much for her brother turning into a zombie because he always treated her like shit when he was left in charge of her after their parents died in a plane crash, like it was her fault that the plane's engine malfunctioned and the plane crashed in Arizona after trying to attempt a landing. She felt more sorry for Spike because sometimes she felt like he was her only friend, except for Tommy, that is, but Tommy isn't as fluffy, and she never wanted to cuddle with Tommy.

After running out the back gate past her zombified brother, she ran smack into Tommy who had been right outside the gate. She grabbed his arm and pulled him as they ran away from her brother who was now hot on their tails. They ran into the tool shed and locked the door as Zach banged on the door and the walls trying to get in. There was a secret storm cellar under the shed and it connected with the sewer tunnels that ran under most of the town. Tommy and Grace escaped through the tunnel, making sure to lock the hatch in the tool shed so Zach couldn't follow them if he happened to get in.

"Ya, sorry, Duff," Tommy said as he patted her on the shoulder. Tommy's story is a little simpler. He lived close to Grace, and when he saw the purple cloud, he got his boots on and was getting ready to leave when he noticed the front door was open and his grandfather was nowhere to be found. Tommy searched the whole house and nope, no Grampa. So he left and headed straight for Grace's when she about barreled into him as she came crashing through the back gate.

As Duff regained her composure, "I wonder if anyone else is here?"

"We were about to go look when you guys came in. We had heard a noise from the first floor because we were sitting on the landing by the door," said Ramsey.

"I don't know if I really wanna go check it out. I mean, if you guys have been here awhile and it's safe, should we stay here?" asked Tommy.

"I thought you said you were hungry?" asked Grace.

"Oh ya! Then lead on, my fellow survivors, for there is food to be found and a stomach growling to satisfy."

"I don't know how you put up with him Grace," commented Duff.

"I really don't know either," Grace retorted, as she gave Tommy a dirty look.

Tommy just looked back at her and blew her a kiss as they walked up the stairs. "So, what was the noise you heard?"

"Not sure, we heard a noise and then a bang, but then we heard the boiler room door open and you guys showed up. So, maybe it was that?" wondered Duff.

Ramsey disagreed. "Naw, the noise came before they opened the boiler door so it couldn't have been them. I think someone came in the front door, and it echoed when they slammed it shut."

Winter of the Hungry

"Well, only one way to find out," advised Grace as they reached the top of the stairs. "Who wants to go through first?" Everyone just looked at each other. "Oh fine! I'll go. What a bunch of chickens." Grace leaned on the door and put her ear against it, hoping to hear something. The door was impossible to hear through unless the noise was quite a bit louder than shuffling feet, but that didn't stop her from trying. The thick basement door was made to withstand any kind of bomb scenario, which was why the tunnels under the town and the school basement were connected. The basement was added onto the school in the 1950s when the Russians had exploded a hydrogen bomb and everyone's anxiety levels were through the roof. The school board at the time wanted to protect the children, if not themselves, and if the tunnels under the city were connected to the school, they could make it all the way to the edge of the island to awaiting boats and paddle to safety.

Grace couldn't hear a thing so she turned the knob ever so

slowly and then waited and listened to see if she heard anything again, just in case someone or something on the other side had seen or heard the doorknob move. Nothing. She opened the door ever so slightly and peeked through the opening, and there stood Dustin, or what used to be Dustin, and he lunged forward knocking Grace back and making the rest of the group, along with Grace and Dustin, fall down the stairs. On the way down Ramsey's neck snapped. Grace only fell about 3/4^{ths} of the way down and Dustin barely missed biting her ankle as he continued to topple on top of the others. Tommy jumped up as soon as he stopped falling and started right back up the stairs not looking back, grabbing Grace's arm and pulling her up. Duff was a little dazed and regaining composure. She saw Dustin getting up off of the floor with an elbow bent in the opposite direction from normal that must have gotten twisted on his way down the stairs. She jumped up trying to pull Ramsey up with her, not realizing that his neck was broken, when Dustin grabbed Ramsey from her arms and started munching down on his stomach contents. Grace had come down the stairs with Tommy in tow to grab Duff and slowly pulled her up the bottom few stairs without alerting Dustin, and then the three of them started to run up the stairs. Dustin noticed them but possibly decided that the meal in front of him was enough and didn't want to chase down more food.

Grace, Tommy, and Duff got to the top of the stairs and slammed the door shut all heaving heavily from the run for their life and turned around to lean against the door and they all screamed. Standing behind them was the gang that had come in through the front door who had heard the commotion and had come over to help.

CHAPTER 9

WINTER OF THE HUNGRY

"Oh my fucking God! You scared the living shit out of us!" cried Duff.

"What the hell is going on? Are you guys okay?" asked Jay as he rushed over to check on them.

"Ya ..." said Grace.

"NO!" cried Duff. "I just lost the love of my life to that sniveling little, I'm-God's-gift-to-women Dustin! (Sob) ... (sob) ..." She turned her head into Grace's shoulder.

As Jay was helping them up off of the floor, "Are any of you bit or scratched?"

"I don't think so," Tommy stated as he looked himself over and then tried to help look Grace over too before she nudged him.

"I'm fine, Tommy," Grace said, annoyed, as she pushed him away.

"Okay, just wanted to double and triple check," he said with a wink.

"Is there anyone else with you guys?" asked Mark.

WINTER OF THE HUNGRY

"Not anymore, it's just the three of us," answered Tommy as Duff sniffed and wiped a tear away.

Jay looked at the door and noticed that there was a deadbolt lock on the outside of the door but it was made to be locked from the inside, not the outside. The deadbolt lock had been installed to keep the kids from going downstairs during school hours and when school wasn't in session. "Do you have the key to this deadbolt, Ann?"

"Ya, actually, I do." Ann walked over to the basement door and pulled out her ring of keys, found the one that belonged to the deadbolt, and locked it. "Now we don't have to worry about anyone else coming through that door; the only way to unlock it is with this key." Holding up the key on her keychain, Ann showed everyone before putting it back on her hip ring. She had all the keys to the school because she worked the most hours and had been there the longest. She got tired of having to contact the principal or the janitor every time she needed in somewhere and finally got permission from the schoolboard to get copies of all the keys. Granted, most of the classrooms were just one master key, but the deadbolt to the basement door and a few others, like the principal's office and the front door were different. "Let's go back to the office," Ann suggested, as she started walking in that direction.

"So, Dustin was here?" I asked.

"Ya," said Grace. She started to tell everyone what exactly happened downstairs, while Duff still sobbed on her shoulder.

"If Dustin was here, that means the Wooly Bully is too, and if he hasn't shown up by now, we have another zombie to keep an eye out for."

Tommy piped up, "Great! I can't stand that guy. Remember when I got sent to his office and he made me stand in the corner with a dunce hat on for chewing gum in Mr. Severson's class?" He looked at Grace. "He even made me wear the gum on my nose! Mr. Severson was such an ass! I never understood why he didn't like gum chewing in his classroom; it's not like it was disturbing."

Ann answered Tommy, "Mr. Severson was old school and believed that you came to school to learn and anything else that got into the way of that was considered unnecessary. Gum is not required to learn, ergo it was unnecessary."

"Ya, well, it was still a stupid rule."

"I'm thinking we need to go floor by floor to see if there are any more zombies here. We can't relax or barricade ourselves anywhere until we know for sure that there aren't any more in the building," suggested Mark.

"I agree. Also, if Dustin and Wooly Bully were here, that means the crew bringing in the lockers could be here too. That's a lot of people unaccounted for," Josh said.

There are three floors plus the basement within the school building, which leaves a lot of hiding places for zombies and possible survivors to hide. The second floor has all the classrooms, the third floor is for all the lab classes so they have the ventilation for the chemicals going directly outside through the ceiling. The gymnasium, cafeteria, and offices are all on the first floor. The gym was at the end of the hallway by walking down three steps and turning a corner, the locker rooms are off of the gym, and the showers are within the locker rooms.

"Okay, let's split up. Itchy, Scarlett, Mark, Josh and Aaron, you guys go down the left side of the hallway, and Tommy, Grace, Josh, Duff, Ann, and I will go down the right side. After you check the rooms, close the blinds, if they aren't already closed, and close the door behind you. This way nothing can walk back in the room without having to open the door. Here are some extra guns. Remember, if you see anything, verify it isn't human and then just shoot for the head," Jay advised.

"How do we verify it isn't human?" Aaron asked.

"Ask it, are you human? And if it doesn't answer yes, then shoot it, duh!" Josh joked.

WINTER OF THE HUNGRY

"That's pretty much what you'll have to do," Jay answered as he put his hand on Aaron's shoulder to keep him from punching Josh. "Haven't seen a zombie talk yet, so I'm assuming they can't. If you don't get a response, shoot." As Jay started to head down the hall, he turned and looked at the group, "And if it's someone you know, remember, they are no longer your friend; your life depends on whether you have the strength to pull that trigger against someone you know."

Josh and I started walking with Mark right behind us, and Scarlett and Aaron in tow. I went into one room and was looking around thinking about how there would never be school again when Scarlett came in the room and the rest of the group continued on to the next room.

"Being in a zombie apocalypse really makes you think, huh?" Scarlett asked me.

"Ya, I was just thinking about never having to go to class again."

WINTER OF THE HUNGRY

"Not exactly what I meant. I love Aaron, but do I really want to be with him when he's so mean to everyone? I don't want to end my life dating the asshole football player. When you are really put into a situation where your life is possibly gonna end, it really makes you re-evaluate your choices ... Aaron is one of mine."

Aaron happened to be still standing outside the door and overheard the conversation. Walking away, he joined Mark in one of the other rooms, "I wish there were more girls alive on this stupid zombie infested island. It would be nice to have some more to hook up with before we all die, ya know?"

"What about Scarlett?"

"Ah, she's just one of those flings, ya know? I'm getting tired of her and just need a little something new." But even as he said it, he knew that she wasn't a fling. He loved her and he didn't want to lose her. Did she really think that he was a horrible person? He just didn't like stupid idiots and told them so; was that so wrong?

Mark retorted, "You should hang on to what you got. With everything that is going on, you really need to hold on to the precious things that are left in life. Most things that we take for granted, we don't realize how important they actually were until they are gone."

Little did Aaron know that Scarlett and I happened to be passing by when he said that, and Scarlett overheard every word. She made the decision there and then, that if she and Aaron survived, she would break up with him. She secretly had feelings for Itchy, and looking at him, realized what a fool she had been for so long because he was nice to everyone and would never treat her like an object like Aaron did. Thinking about this just heated her up, and she decided she wasn't waiting for if she survived or not; she was breaking it off now. "You bastard!" Scarlett shouted as she walked into the room, startling Mark and Aaron. "You can go to hell, and if we find anymore girls, I'll be sure to send them your way, alive or dead! We are through!" She took off his class ring and threw it across the room and stormed out through the door.

"Looks like you should have kept your mouth shut, Aaron," Josh snickered, who had happened to show up just in time to hear the whole conversation. "At least that way, you could have still have gotten laid before you died, but now, you just screwed yourself, literally." Laughing, he walked up to the window, "Hey, come here, Aaron," Josh beckoned.

Aaron walked up, and in an annoyed tone, "What?"

"Look at those beauties down there; you could go screw with them, they'd be so grateful to get a bite out of you!" Josh laughed as he and Mark left the room, leaving Aaron alone in the room to hang his head watching a few female zombies lumber around the school yard.

The survivors checked all of the first floor including the gym and the locker rooms and met back up in the office and said that the first floor was secure.

WINTER OF THE HUNGRY

"It's getting dark," Tommy pointed out as he looked at the fact that he could barely see anyone anymore.

"Well, I don't want to turn the lights on because that could attract zombies from outside, so I'm not turning the backups on either. We will just have to make do with the flashlights that are in every classroom," answered Jay.

"How are we gonna prevent any zombies that may be up on the other floors from coming down the stairs?" asked Duff.

Looking around, Josh saw the returnables in the corner of the office. "How about we take all the cans from the return box and set them up on the 2nd floor landing? That way if anything comes down the stairs they'd end up kicking the cans and we'd hear them coming."

"That's an awesome idea, Josh," Ann said as she passed him to get the box.

There were two sets of stairs, one at each end of the hall, so the group split up, each taking an armful of cans and set them up on the landing in various patterns so anyone walking through them would have to hit at least one, especially if they weren't paying attention. The one thing the group forgot, though ... was the elevator. It wasn't used unless a student or faculty member had an injury or if there was something too big to haul up the stairs, but either way, the group didn't think to check it, just in case.

After the cans were set up, Tommy, Grace, and Duff decided that they wanted to take a shower and clean up because of being in the tunnels under the town and wrestling with Dustin. Especially Duff, she just needed that time to relax and let the hot water take her away, if even for a moment. They all went down to the locker rooms and Duff showered first as Grace and Tommy kept an eye out at the door. Duff thought to herself, as the steamy shower rinsed her off, that she would never find another love like Ramsey. It just wasn't fair, why did it have to be him?

Grace came in because Duff had started crying, "Don't worry about anything else right now, Duff. Just take a shower,

WINTER OF THE HUNGRY

calm down, we'll get a good night's sleep, get to the boat launch and leave this horrible mess behind us. You'll meet someone new, and I know that's not what you want to hear, but it will happen. You'll have a tragic story to tell your new love someday and it'll be all behind us."

"I know, it's just that I'd be leaving Ramsey too. It's just not fair. What did I ever do in my life to deserve to be ripped away from the one good thing I had in my life?" She bowed her head back under the water and continued to clean up. Duff finished her shower and pulled some extra clothes out of her locker that she kept there just in case she wanted to go to the local pizzeria right after school. Gym was her last period of the day so she didn't want to be smelly when she and Ramsey went to eat, so she always kept a spare set of clothes at school. After dressing, "I'm gonna go find the others and figure out the sleeping arrangements, I just want this day over."

Grace watched Duff walk away, "She is gonna have a

really hard time getting over Ramsey. Oh well, one step at a time.
Keep an eye on the door, Tommy, while I clean up?"

"Sure," he answered winking.

"Don't even get any ideas."

"Who? Me? Never," he snickered.

Jay and the rest of us were working to find some kind of power switch that didn't turn the lights on but got the stove and fridge going again so everyone could eat. We were all in the cafeteria waiting to see if we could whip up some food before bed. Little did we know that while we were messing with the switches, the elevator backup power was on the same circuit as the kitchen so the food wouldn't spoil and nobody would get stuck in the elevator. When Jay hit the switch that got the kitchen back up and running it also turned the power on for the elevator. The door to elevator opened and out limped Principal Wooley. He had been stuck in the elevator when the power was knocked out by a truck hitting the power grid box after swerving to miss an ambulance.

WINTER OF THE HUNGRY

The ambulance had been driving in the wrong lane because the passenger being brought to the hospital decided to wake from the dead and eat the driver. Principal Wooley had been trying to hide in the elevator from one of the crew members that brought in the new lockers but didn't make it in time. He was bitten before the doors closed and while locked inside had passed on and came back as something even more deadly than what I described as a mean principal.

The cafeteria was on the opposite end of the hall from the gym and the principal was wandering around the small corridor by the elevator, so when Duff walked by talking to herself she didn't see or hear the zombie principal limping around, but he heard her and started moving in her direction. Duff walked to the cafeteria to get something to eat, not knowing what was following her. Tommy was always hungry and Grace was poking fun at him that he had to wait until she showered before he could follow Duff and go eat, and the sounds from the conversation echoed enough that

WINTER OF THE HUNGRY

Principal Wooley heard them and started wandering in the direction of the gym and the lockers rooms instead of following Duff all the way to the cafeteria.

The cafeteria doors were double and swung open like an old doorway on an old saloon, which also means that they didn't lock. Everyone except Grace and Tommy were in the cafeteria, laughing, talking, and every once in a while I would stop just to listen for cans rattling.

"So what are we gonna eat? What's on the menu, Jay?" Duff asked.

"It's Taco Tuesday!!" yelled Josh. "Yummy! Are there any tacos, Jay?"

As Jay looked into the refrigerator, he saw that most of the food was still salvageable, as the fridge kept it cold even though the power wasn't on. "Well, we have stuff to make tacos and there's mashed potatoes and then some gravy looking thing ..."

"Ugh, no way," interrupted Josh. "That's Monday

WINTER OF THE HUNGRY

Surprise. I told you that lunch lady kept the food to poison us week to week," he stated, as he pointed at me.

Josh couldn't stand the food at the school, except for Taco Tuesdays. He said you could at least see what was in the taco before you ate it. All the other food was stuff all mixed together, and he figured the lunch lady was hired by people who hate children to exterminate them all like bugs, so adults could be free from the responsibilities of being an adult. Josh had some hair-brained ideas, but even Tommy hated Monday Surprise, and that was saying something.

"Okay, so tacos it is," Jay pulled the ingredients out of the fridge and put them on the counter. "The microwave is on the same circuit at the stove so we can each make a plate and heat it up. But keep an ear out for cans because the noise from the microwave might be loud enough to bring some zombies our way."

"Do you think we should wait until after we check the rest of the building before we eat?" asked Scarlett.

Winter of the Hungry

"You know, you're probably right. Should we wait for Grace and Tommy to get back before we go check?"

Rolling her eyes, Grace answered annoyingly, "They probably are showering together, so I don't think so. I'll wait here anyway; I don't want to go looking for more zombies, especially now that it's so dark and we only have flashlights to see."

"I'll wait with her too," Scarlett joined in. "I'm really tired and probably wouldn't see one if it was in front of my face. I can barely keep my eyes open."

"Alright," Jay agreed. "But you have to keep a gun for safety. Just listen for the cans or any other gunfire and be at the ready, just in case." He handed Scarlett one of his silencer guns and walked out into the hall with the rest of the group. "We'll split up and head up both sets of stairs; I'll take the second floor with Mark and Itchy. Josh and Aaron, you go with Ann to the third floor. Take this set of stairs up and come down the other set. We'll do the opposite so all areas are secure."

WINTER OF THE HUNGRY

As we walked down the hallway to the set of stairs by the gym, we didn't see Principal Wooly as he was already in the gym and on his way into the locker rooms were Tommy and Grace were. Principal Wooly heard the sounds that we was making and was about to turn around, but Tommy was being so loud about being hungry that in the end Wooly Bully kept heading toward the two unsuspecting victims.

Tommy was sitting outside the locker room and finally stopped complaining about being hungry because he knew the longer he complained, the longer Grace would take in the shower on purpose just to annoy him. Grace started humming to herself and Tommy turned around and tried to peek through the door to catch a glimpse of Grace in her natural beauty. While humming, Grace thought to herself how nice it would be to be with someone that actually loved her. It wouldn't have been so bad with Tommy if sex wasn't the only thing that fueled his brain. She just couldn't see herself with Tommy for the rest of her life on Earth, no matter how short that may be. To be with someone who only wanted sex and not a true relationship. Although, Tommy made her feel that she was better than what she thought she was, and he did treat her like a queen at times. While Tommy was trying to peek in on Grace, Principal Wooly was sneaking up on Tommy. He ended up biting him on the back of the neck which rendered Tommy unable to scream and just made gurgling noises instead.

Grace yelled from the shower, "Knock it off, Tommy! This is no time to be making fake zombies noises to try and scare me."

Principal Wooly, hearing Grace's yells, stopped eating out Tommy's throat and headed into the shower area. There was no shower barrier around the shower stall so Principal Wooly was able to meander right in, pushing on the shower curtain as he did so.

"Tommy, I'm serious! You are NOT funny!"

Wooly Bully kept walking toward Grace and as he did the shower curtain slipped off of him to reveal to Grace it wasn't

WINTER OF THE HUNGRY

Tommy joking around. She attempted to run out of the shower away from the zombie and slipped on the wet floor, grabbing the shower curtain on her way down and fell and hit her head and knocked herself out. Wooly Bully started eating her as zombie Tommy wandered into the shower stall and joined in eating his best friend and love of his life.

All that could be heard was the sucking and smacking of eating of flesh that was partially masked by the sounds of the shower stall and the water hitting the floor, shower curtain, and surround area. No shouts for help were called out to warn the remaining members of the group that danger was lurking in the area.

CHAPTER 10

WINTER OF THE HUNGRY

While we searched the school, Scarlett and Duff hung out in the cafeteria talking about what was going on and wondering how much longer Grace and Tommy were going to be. The cafeteria was like any other school cafeteria with brick walls and big windows, which we had closed when we came in. There were tables and chairs everywhere for the kids to sit at and along the right side of the room from the door was the kitchen area which had the standard chrome piping for the kids to put their trays on as they walked through the food bar picking which foods they wanted.

Each day there was a set schedule of what the kids would get to eat. Monday, already pointed out by Josh, was a surprise. It was actually just chicken, mashed potatoes, corn, and gravy all mixed together. I wouldn't admit it to Josh, but I actually liked Mondays. Tuesday was tacos, Wednesday was Weiner Wednesday, which Principal Wooly hated it being called, but the kids just continued calling it that, so he had to deal with it.

WINTER OF THE HUNGRY

Thursday was Thirsty Thursday; it was a special day because the cafeteria served canned pop with lunch that day. The food would be whatever was sent extra that week and ranged from hamburgers to chicken Caesar salad. Fridays were the best though, Friday was always pizza day. Even during Lent, pizza was served but the Catholics could have fish sandwiches if they chose to. Tuesdays and Fridays were the only two days that Josh didn't complain about the food. But he always found something to complain about in its place. Josh swore that the lunch lady was a skinny little old biddy that lived in the back of the lunch room when school wasn't in session.

"I wonder what's taking them so long. Do you think we ought to go and check on them?" asked Scarlett.

"I don't know. I think we should stay here."

"We would hear the cans if anyone was coming. I think we should go and see."

"Okay, but if I walk in on them having sex, I'm totally

gonna punch you."

"Deal."

Scarlett and Duff left the cafeteria and started walking down the hallway towards the gym. As they got closer to the gym doors they heard sucking noises and sloshing noises.

"I hope that's not what I think it is," whispered Duff.

"How would have a zombie got by us without us knowing? We checked the whole first floor."

Slowly Duff and Scarlett looked around the corner of the wall into the gym and saw Principal Wooly and Tommy with his neck half ripped out, wandering around the gym.

"Oh no!" sobbed Duff. "Not again. Why do I keep losing people? And where's Grace?"

"Ssh, or you're gonna let them know we are here. I'm a pretty good aim, so I'm gonna shoot them with the silencer, and we'll tell everyone when they get back what happened, okay? But you gotta keep quiet so they don't come this way."

WINTER OF THE HUNGRY

"Okay."

Scarlett took aim, and was a little shaky but shot Tommy and the Principal right in the head. "Come on, we need to find Grace."

As they walked closer to the showers the sloshing noise got louder and they found Grace, who couldn't walk because Wooly Bully and Tommy had eaten her middle and she was in two pieces. She was attempting to move around by her hands, her innards and intestines behind her. She had only made it out of the shower stall and into the locker room and the trail of innards and blood led back to the shower stalls. Scarlett walked over and shot her in the head.

"We are gonna have to look around and see if there are any other zombies around because we don't know where Wooly Bully came from."

"Let's clean this up; I don't want anyone else to see this."

Duff and Scarlett hauled all the bodies to this back fire escape door that was always latched from the inside, and slowly opened it to peer out to see if it was safe. There were no zombies near enough to be worrisome, and so they threw the bodies out the door and relatched it. There was still a lot of blood but there was nothing to really clean it up with. Besides, there really wasn't time to be sensitive about the sight of blood.

Scarlett looked really pale and worn out at this point, and Duff asked her, "Are you feeling all right?"

"Ya, just a little tired from hauling bodies of people I know around. That's six now that I had to do today. I need a vacation."

Unbeknownst to Duff, that wasn't the only reason Scarlett looked worn out. They walked back to the cafeteria and put a couple of tables together so Scarlett could lie down, while Duff sat in a chair looking out the window contemplating the point of even trying to survive in a zombie apocalypse; she just didn't see one.

Ann came through the door, "Third floor is done. Josh and Aaron went to help Jay, Mark, and Itchy." And then she saw the blood, and Scarlett lying down. "Are you guys okay?"

WINTER OF THE HUNGRY

"Ssh, she's sleeping. Ya, we're fine. Principal Wooly was somewhere on the first floor and found Tommy and Grace in the showers. Scarlett and I went to find them after you guys went upstairs and Wooly Bully and Tommy were in the gym. Grace was still in the showers; she was in two pieces!" Duff exclaimed as she started bawling into Ann's sleeve.

"Aww, honey, I'm sorry."

"Scarlett shot them and we threw the bodies outside but didn't have anything to clean up the blood with. I'm so tired of losing people; what is the point of this? Is there any reason to survive when every five minutes someone else is dead?"

Duff's head was still in Ann's sleeve so she didn't see Scarlett get up off of the table and start heading towards them ...

Meanwhile upstairs ...

"I've never wanted school food so bad before. I'm telling ya, that lunch lady monster puts all this crap probably from other countries into our food," Josh told Jay and Aaron. "All that illegal stuff that we aren't supposed to ingest like lead."

"Just because you can't pronounce it doesn't mean that it's from another country," said Aaron.

"You can't even pronounce your own name," snapped Josh.

"You know I'm sick and tired of you and your sarcastic mouth, cutting me down and shit."

"Like you're the nicest person in the world? You say everything that's on your mind and you pick on everyone. You're an idiot. You are the stereotype of a jock, you're mean, and you only care about yourself."

"Knock it off, you two, you are gonna get us killed with your arguing," Jay interrupted. "Now is not the time for immaturity."

Aaron asked Jay, "You have Government Greens on; are you military?"

"No, I work at the testing site, or well, I used to."

"Do you know what's going on?"

WINTER OF THE HUNGRY

"Sort of but sort of don't."

"Well, whatever it is, they are not coming to get us," interrupted Josh.

"Why is that?" asked Jay.

"When we picked up Mark, they had reconnaissance planes fly over and we heard on his walkie that they couldn't stop to pick us up because of possible contaminants."

Aaron asked, "So it's possible that even if we do get off the island, the government probably won't even let us set foot on dry land?

"Probably shoot us on sight," answered Josh.

"Great! Just great."

"Ssh, what was that?"

"Oh, shut up."

"No, I'm serious."

Jay shooshed them both, "Stay back against the wall, and be quiet!"

"I don't know where they are," came a voice from down the hall.

"Itchy?"

"Ya!" I answered. "Where are you guys?"

Josh jumped up and down like he was doing jumping jacks, "We're over here, see?"

Aaron looked at Jay, "He's such an idiot. I hope he gets eaten."

"No, you don't. The more people that get eaten, the less chance you have at survival."

"Ya, whatever."

"What are you guys doing up here? Where's Ann?"

"We finished the third floor; there was nobody up there. Ann went back down by the girls. We watched her go to the cafeteria so she's safe. We came back up here to help you guys, just in case," Mark answered.

There were new lockers all over the second floor lying on

the ground, and some old ones too; which meant the crew that brought in the lockers was around somewhere. It looked like they had been in the process of replacing them when the dust happened. Some of crew had to have been outside and someone had to have been letting them in since the back door automatically shuts by itself. They must have opened the door for an infected crew member and whoever had been watching the door must have gotten bit or scratched and went back up to the second floor to inform the rest of the crew and the infection spread.

"There were three delivery trucks outside that I could see and if you figure two guys per van that would be six zombies that might be in here," I stated.

"Aren't you a ray of sunshine with the information?" Aaron snapped.

"Well, we don't know how many are outside and how many are inside, so they may not all be inside."

"Still not helpful."

WINTER OF THE HUNGRY

"Do you hear that?" Mark asked as they got near one of the rooms.

"It sounds like a kid crying," Jay whispered. The sound got louder as we checked the classrooms. The third door down we found a little kid hiding behind a bookcase. When the door opened the crying stopped. "Is someone in here?"

"I'm here," said a little voice. "Are ... are you one of them? Or ... or are you human?"

"I'm human; are you okay?" Jay asked as the kid came out from behind the bookcase.

He kind of stopped short when he saw Mark in the doorway with one arm, and Mark reassured him, "Oh, don't worry about my arm. I lost it many years ago in the war. No zombie took it from me."

"I want my mommy," cried the scared child.

"Who's his mom? Does anyone know who this kid is?" asked Jay as he looked down at the child that was now hugging him.

"My mom's a teacher in this room."

"His mom is Ms. Argo," I answered. Bending down I asked the kid, "Was she here with you?"

"I don't know if she's here. Nobody was at my house when I woke up from my nap, and so I left my mom a note, like I'm supposed to when I go somewhere, and rode my bike here to find her. There were these people that were scary and I was so scared and I rode as fast as I could to get here and ran inside to this room, but she wasn't here, but I was so scared I didn't wanna go back outside so I hid," he stated, all in one breath.

"Okay, is there anyone else, your dad maybe?" Jay asked

"No, it's just me and my mom, and I don't know where she is."

I stood up, "We have to check the rest of these rooms. I'll stay here with, hey, what's your name, kid?"

"Caleb."

WINTER OF THE HUNGRY

"I'll stay here with Caleb and you guys go check the other rooms so we can get back down to the girls."

"Okay, shut the door behind us and we'll be right back." Jay turned and the others followed him as I closed and locked the door behind them.

Caleb was only waist high to Jay and had red hair and freckles all over his face. I assumed he looked like his dad because Ms. Argo had black hair and no freckles at all. "What grade are you in Caleb?"

"2nd."

"We're gonna stay really quiet, okay, Caleb? And those guys, my friends, are gonna go make sure there are no other scary people on this floor, okay?"

"Okay."

"So, what are we gonna do with a kid?" asked Josh standing in the hallway. "How do we keep him safe?"

"We'll have to do the best that we can, and if we can't find his mom, the plan won't change. We'll get to the edge of the island to the boats and head for the mainland and take him with us," advised Mark.

"We'll have to leave a note here for her, just in case, so if she comes here looking for him, she'll know where to look," suggested Jay.

"Good idea," agreed Aaron.

As they continued on down the hallway, they started to hear unnatural moaning noises coming from one of the classrooms and saw blood smeared all over the floor as if something had been dragged in or out from another room. There were also bloody hand prints on the door way. Sneaking up on the door and peering in, Jay saw two men dressed in professional gear and deemed they were some of the locker crew. One of the men had a broken foot and was limping around the room on his ankle and some of his jaw was missing. The other guy had a bloody spot soaked through his shirt on his back left shoulder blade, but since he was facing in the

WINTER OF THE HUNGRY

opposite direction, Jay couldn't see his face to see if he was human

or not. He looked back at the group and held up two fingers

indicating there were two people in the room. He leaned forward

and aimed at the one that was facing him and fired, hitting him in

the neck. A gurgle of noise came from the shot crew member,

whose nametag said 'Bob'. Bob then started towards the door and

the other crew member turned where Jay could finally see his face,

and it was a girl.

Her nametag read 'Olive'. One eye was missing and some

veins were hanging from the socket. She also started towards the

door upon hearing the noise. Jay took aim again, this time

standing in the doorway since they both had seen him anyway, and

shot. The bullet went straight through Bob's head and hit Olive in

the missing eye hole. As the bullet exited the back of Olive's

head, it splattered brain matter on the desks behind her and she hit

a few desks and knocked them over as she fell.

This alerted the other crew members that had still been

WINTER OF THE HUNGRY

inside the building, and they started to come out into the hall.

There were only two, one of whom had a chunk missing out of his

leg and moved pretty slowly. The other one was a little faster, not

having any visible signs, and was upon them faster than they could

move. Aaron punched it in the face, but to no avail and Mark shot

it in the head as Jay and Josh tried to hold it back as it kept trying

to bite Aaron. By that time, the slow moving one had caught up

and Aaron grabbed the gun out of Mark's hand. "Screw you,

zombie asshole," he said, and shot him in the face three times, the

third one actually puncturing the brain.

Bending over, catching his breath, "Jesus, that one was

fast," Josh stated.

"Wait, I hear something," Jay whispered.

"Uh, guys, there are legs in this room with the two that we

shot. So, where's the other half?" Mark asked.

They followed the blood trail into the other classroom and

found the other half of the body, wiggling on the floor trying to get around. Josh walked up to it and said, "Sorry, buddy," and hit it in the head with the axe.

After checking the rest of the rooms, the guys decided that there must have been only five crew members inside at the time, or maybe one of the vans had only had one person in it. They didn't find any other zombies, so they headed back to the classroom where Caleb and I sat waiting.

Knocking, "Okay Itchy, it's safe to come out now," Josh said.

Opening the door I said, "Okay, I heard a lot of scuffling, how many did you guys get?" Looking down the hallway I saw the two bodies of the ones that had attacked them and decided to wait to let Caleb come out of the room. "Wanna shove them in a room so he don't have to see them?"

"Ya, gimmie a hand, Josh." Jay walked over, and they picked up the two bodies and threw them into the room with the other two and the bottom half of the one. "It's safe to come out now."

"We decided we were gonna leave a note in the room for your mom, Caleb, so that way she knows where you are if she comes looking for you, because we're going to go to the boat dock and head to the mainland. Okay? We can't leave you here alone," Josh said as he bent down to look him in the eye.

"Okay."

Josh and Caleb walked back into the room and left a note for Ms. Argo, and Josh let Caleb sign his name so she would know that the note was real. They taped it to the door and closed it. That way it would be the first thing she saw if she came here looking for him.

"Let's go back downstairs now and get something to eat. I'm starving," complained Josh.

"Me too," said Caleb.

"... and then the blond said, 'Well, that's not my car!'" Josh exclaimed as he and the group came walking back into the cafeteria. Everyone was laughing at Josh's joke, but suddenly stopped when they saw the horrific sight before their eyes. Scarlett had turned while they were gone. Unbeknownst to the group, she had gotten scratched by Stacey Hanson when they first arrived in the school and had died in her sleep while lying on the tables. Duff was lying on the floor with her face half missing and Scarlett was next to her with a bullet in her head. Ann stood there and continued looking down at the bodies while Jay tried to get her attention.

"Honey? You okay? What happened?"

Ann had had her back to Scarlett and was the first one to be bit and her fighting nature kicked in a little too late. Ann ended up on the floor with a massive chunk taken out of her neck, her carotid artery bleeding faster than she could stop it, she was getting dizzy and blacking out but found enough strength to shoot Scarlet in the side of the temple as she was eating Duff's face. Duff didn't even have time to understand what was happening before she died.

WINTER OF THE HUNGRY

Ann had awaked zombiefied and had just finished making a meal out of the rest of Duff's face when she heard the sounds of the group coming closer. She was quicker than the others as she wasn't missing any limbs, and Jay screamed as Ann looked up at him with blood on her face and dead black eyes. "NO!"

As Ann moved closer to the five remaining members, Jay grabbed his gun, shot Ann right between the eyes, and put his gun back to his side all in one smooth move like something out of a movie. Josh, I, and Mark all turned to look at Aaron and Jay who were standing silently, staring at both of the women they loved. Jay turned and walked away from the cafeteria and down the hall. I started to go after him, but Mark stopped him. "Let him go, he needs time."

"We can't afford time right now, and we definitely can't afford for anyone to be splitting the group up anymore. Every time we do, we lose more people. Pretty soon there won't be anyone left on this island to survive." I turned and ran down the hall after

Winter of the Hungry

Jay.

"What the hell just happened? I mean what the hell?" asked Josh. "How in the hell did everyone just turn into a zombie? I mean how?"

"I don't know. But we need to figure that out," Mark answered as he walked up to Ann.

"Be careful!"

"She's dead, don't worry," Mark reassured Josh as he looked Ann over. "It looks like Ann was bit in the throat." He walked over to Duff. "Duff was, well, eaten ... and still a zombie, shit!" Duff had grabbed Mark's boot and was attempting to get up off of the floor when Mark shot her in the head. "Jesus Christ! I've had my share of heart attacks today. My God!" Mark turned and looked at Scarlett, "Seems she was shot in the head. Must have been when she tried attacking Ann, she shot her, but not before she was bitten. Then Ann must have eaten Duff. But how did Scarlett turn?" Mark removed her collar and saw nothing and then lifted both her sleeves and saw that her arm on the right side had a big black mark on it that might have originally been a scratch, but was infected very badly. "She must have gotten scratched when we first got here by that zombie that got her arm in the door."

"Um, where are Tommy and Grace? They should have been back by now," Aaron asked as he walked over to Scarlett.

"That's a good question; let's go find them, but first we need to get Itchy and Jay back with us. Itchy was right in that we shouldn't split up anymore."

The boys walked down the hall to find me and Jay. We were sitting in a classroom and Jay was just staring down at the floor. "I can't believe that I shot her. We just got back together; I was gonna make it up to her. Make up the fact that our marriage was so bad for a while. I didn't want a divorce, she was my moon, my stars, my everything! I loved her so very much; how could I just shoot her without even blinking?"

WINTER OF THE HUNGRY

"You didn't have a choice and you cared so much for her that you didn't want her to suffer and continue on like that. I wouldn't want anyone I love to be a zombie." I turned and looked at the wall. I was thinking of Scarlett and how much I had loved her. I wished I would have told her, had I known. That's when I saw the guys in the doorway.

Mark interrupted my train of thought, "We figured out what happened but Grace and Tommy aren't back yet, so there's still more people to find, but we wanted everyone together before we went to the gym."

Getting up out of the desk, Jay wiped his eyes, "Ya, okay, I gotta keep going for Ann. Plus, I still need to find my mom and Joe. Seems like we may not be able to stay here for much longer."

Walking down the hallway to the gym, the guys listened for noises and heard nothing. As they walked in they saw the trails of blood leading out the back fire escape. Mark opened it slowly and saw what was left of Grace, Tommy, and Principal Wooly.

WINTER OF THE HUNGRY

"Tommy and Grace are back here but there's another guy too."

Josh looked out the door, "That's Wooly Bully! Where the hell was he hiding?"

Mark relocked the door. "That's a good question. We checked all the floors and even the first floor. Was there somewhere that we didn't look? Another room that only staff use or something?"

"The elevator!" I exclaimed. "When we were switching on breakers for the stove and kitchen stuff, I bet we kicked on the elevator. I betcha Wooly Bully was in there and got out when the doors opened."

"Sonofabitch! That jackass!" shouted Josh. "If he wasn't already dead, I'd kill him!"

CHAPTER 11

WINTER OF THE HUNGRY

"Well, that's just fucking great! Now what do we do?" asked Josh.

"Josh, knock it off," I said as he nodded in Jay's direction. "Plus, watch your language," as I looked down at Caleb.

"Well, I guess there really is no point in staying here anymore. I mean, it's safe and all but anyone else notice how cold it got over the last hour or two?" Josh asked.

"Ya, according to Ann the backup generator wasn't connected to the heat. If the heat went out, the school board just figured on sending the kids home if it was during a school day." He started to walk back towards the entrance to the gym, "Looks like we should get what food we can in our stomachs and head over to The N&P Store; they will at least have heat," suggested Jay.

"How do you know that?" asked Aaron, puzzled.

"The N&P has their heat connected to the backup generator so if the power ever went out, none of the food would spoil no

WINTER OF THE HUNGRY

matter what the weather. That way if it was hot out, the food that needed to be room temperature would remain so, and same went for the cold. I used to work there when I was a teenager and the power went out because of a bad storm and I was mad because we couldn't go home. I just remember my mom calling the store every 15 minutes asking if I was able to leave yet because she was so worried about me not being home. Pissed my boss off to the point where he finally sent me home, and then fired me the next day."

"Nice, who was your boss?" asked Mark as they walked back to the cafeteria.

"Decker Pinn."

"That old coot that sits in the back and glares at everyone? Holy crap, that guy must be 150 years old!" exclaimed Josh. "He always looks at me funny when I'm in there. Like I'm gonna steal something."

"Probably do," Aaron accused.

Winter of the Hungry

"Do not! I never stole a thing in my life. I can't believe you worked for that guy. He's a jerk. Must be related to Aaron."

"Oh, shut up, dickwad!"

"Knock it off, you two, NOW!" shouted Jay as he pushed through the swinging doors of the cafeteria. "I'm so sick of you two fighting. Grow the fuck up. People are dying all around us, and you two keep fighting like it's just any other day. I just shot my fucking wife because she turned into a zombie. I don't know who else is alive out there, but I swear to God that if you two don't knock it the hell off, I will shoot you both just for the peace and quiet!"

Jay stormed off into the back and started slamming plates and pots around to make himself something to eat while mumbling under his breath every few minutes and shaking his head. "Wow, what a jerk." Looking from Jay to Josh, Aaron turned and went and sat in the corner of the room and just stared at the floor where Scarlett lay, wondering if it would have mattered if he had treated her differently. Wondering if everything she and Josh had been saying all night was true. Was he really that much of an asshole?

"Someone's ragging it," kidded Josh.

"Knock it off, Josh," I punched him in the shoulder. "Don't you know when to quit?"

"Nope, that's what makes my personality so warm and fuzzy." He smiled a big smile.

It was no wonder I could never stay mad at him. He was just too dorky to be mad at. I walked toward the kitchen to fix myself a plate, "We should all eat. I don't know when we'll be able to eat again. The heat may be on at N&P but that doesn't mean that there aren't zombies all over it or it's been raided or something. Might as well eat now."

Usually Jay was a calm person, but he had no patience for kids. Didn't know how Ann handled it day in and day out. He stopped banging around things long enough to mourn his wife. What was he gonna do without her. Knowing her, she'd probably tell him to keep going for the sake of humanity or some shit like that, but even though it was cheesy, he knew that she'd be right. He came out of the kitchen, "Look, I'm sorry, guys."

"It's understandable, Jay," Mark said as he patted his shoulder. "You're entitled to an outburst because of the situation, but we need you ... we need to all keep our heads or we have no chance at survival. We need to keep going for the ones we lost."

"You're right, let's eat and then we need to figure out how to head over to N&P, but we can't eat in here," he said, looking at Caleb who was still standing in the hallway behind me.

We decided to eat in the office since they knew that room was not covered in the blood of their friends. After we all had filled our stomachs and our backpacks with what food we could find, we started to devise a plan to get from the school to the N&P safely.

"Well, if we go through the back through the door off the gym, there weren't hardly any zombies back there," suggested

WINTER OF THE HUNGRY

Josh.

"But if we go that way, we'd have to go straight across the back parking lot of the school to get on the road that leads to the N&P," countered Mark. "That's a pretty wide open space to be vulnerable in."

"But when I looked outside there was one of those vans outside from the delivery crew. We could take one of those and drive straight to N&P and park right next to the front door," Josh countered back.

"We should go back up to the third floor and make sure none of those crew members have keys on them, because that would really suck to run out there to get into the van and then there are no keys," Aaron said with more than a little bit of a huff.

Jay agreed, "Sounds like an idea. I'll run up there and check and be right back down. We already cleared that area so we don't all need to go."

"Ya, but even though we cleared it, you shouldn't go alone.

WINTER OF THE HUNGRY

I'll go with you," I offered. "Just in case."

As Jay and I went back up to the third floor to get the keys, Aaron, Josh, Mark, and Caleb were left in the office to wait. Aaron was not talking to Josh, and Josh wasn't talking to Aaron, Mark was enjoying the silence, and Caleb kept looking between the three of them and then at the floor. He was the first to speak, "I hate waiting in the Principal's office. Always feels like I'm gonna get in trouble for something I didn't do." He swung his legs back and forth from under the chair.

"Ya, still get that same feeling of dread I got when I had to wait for Wooly Bully to come out and he always said the same thing, 'You again?' I hated that." Josh rolled his eyes. "I didn't get in trouble that much."

"I'm sure," mumbled Aaron under his breath, too low for anyone to hear him.

All of a sudden there was a clanging of cans, and all four jumped.

WINTER OF THE HUNGRY

"Caleb, stay here!" shouted Josh as he, Mark, and Aaron ran out the door, shutting it behind them.

Caleb ran and hid under the principal's desk.

"What the hell was that?" asked Josh as he, Mark, and Aaron ran down the hall to the stairs.

A couple of cans were rolling in the hallway, and Aaron and Josh slowed down to see what was coming. Apparently Dustin and Ramsey had been pawing at the back of the basement door, and eventually one of them had hit the bolt lock just enough that it eventually unlocked. They had been hearing the group talk and wanted desperately to get beyond that door. The door crept open enough for Ramsey to get his fingers in and pull the door the rest of the way through so he and Dustin could get out. They started wandering through the halls, Ramsey a little slower than Dustin, and because the boys in the office weren't making any noise, they followed the voices up the stairs. When Aaron, Mark, and Josh turned the corner, they saw Dustin about half way up, but Ramsey was having a hard time making it and was falling all over the cans, sending them rolling down the stairs. All of a sudden, they started making growling noises and in the next second each had two bullets in his head.

Standing at the top of the stairs were Jay and I holding our guns out in front of us looking like something from out of a movie shoot scene. "That was cool!" shouted Josh.

"We heard the cans and saw those two headed up the stairs; how'd they get out?" I asked.

"Don't know. Maybe one of them unlocked the door?" Aaron suggested.

Josh wanted to make a smart aleck remark but thought better of it. "Only way they could have gotten out I guess is if one of them did."

All of a sudden there were growls and grunts and groans coming from behind the guys on the first floor. Jay and I ran down the stairs, and as we turned the corner, we saw that there had been

Winter of the Hungry

a few others that had had the idea of wandering the tunnels under the town and apparently turned while trying to find refuge. Now that the basement door was open, there were about five of them coming down the hall. In front of them was a girl running. "RUN!" she shouted as she headed toward them.

"Caleb's still in the office!" shouted Josh as he ran up to the girl and inside the office and shouted for Caleb. "Caleb, we gotta leave now!"

Caleb came out from under the desk and ran to Josh, and they both ran out the office doors just as the five man zombie herd came lumbering toward them. One had a butcher knife stuck in his shoulder, another didn't have a shirt and had a few gunshots in the stomach, another one looked like someone had ripped his jaw out, the fourth one was wearing a football jersey and was missing an arm, and the last one was female and had a carving fork sticking out of her neck. None of them were dressed for outside weather, so they had to have followed the girl down into the tunnels.

WINTER OF THE HUNGRY

As they ran down the hallway, Jay shouted, "To the back door!"

We ran into the gym, and I got to the door first and unlatched it. We had enough time to be careful and make sure it was safe to go outside before we all flew out the door and into one of the vans. What we didn't figure was that missing crew member might still be in the van. I pulled open the door and out fell the other crew member. I punched him in the head and jumped into the van along with the rest of the group by opening the back doors and jumping in and shutting the doors as I was already driving away.

As everyone caught their breath, the girl breathed out a "Thank you."

"You're welcome, but where did you come from?" asked Jay.

"I was in the tunnels looking to get to the boat dock but got turned around so I went up, and that's when the zombies saw me and followed me down. I got to the door in the basement and opened it only to find there were two zombies already in there. I quietly listened to see how far behind me the others were. I waited because the one kept hitting the lock mechanism, and I knew it was only a matter of time before he unlocked it. Only problem was that there was no way out besides past the group following me, so I was stuck waiting. I was hoping he hit the lock before the other ones found me. I had waited a few minutes after they had gotten out before I came out. The door was so noisy that I didn't want them to hear it and come back in and then I'd really be stuck, so I didn't move the door. I snuck up the stairs and saw them turn to go up the stairs, and that's when I heard the zombies that were behind me come through. I tried shutting the door, but there was no lock, and then I saw you guys."

"Who are you?" Aaron asked?

"Name's Carron, just moved here about a month ago, now I wish I hadn't."

WINTER OF THE HUNGRY

Carron was an average looking girl, normal features with short blond hair, but her eyes, her eyes seemed to pop out of her head they were so big. They weren't freaky big, but it was the first thing that anyone would notice about her; those big green eyes. She was about four foot ten and was kind of roly poly, but you knew she must be doing some kind of athletics since she was running pretty fast down the school hallway.

"Where did you move from?" Aaron wondered.

"Oregon. My family gave me money for college and I decided to go to Middleton University on the mainland. I thought it would be cool to live on the island and take the ferry over when I had class. I'm from a small town so I thought I would feel more comfortable on the island than in the city; just never figured I'd be fighting for my life to get off the island."

"It's usually a great town, we may just be having an off day is all," Josh joked.

"Well, welcome to the group Carron. That's Itchy driving

WINTER OF THE HUNGRY

..." I waved and looked in the rearview. "... Josh ..." pointing to Josh in the passenger seat who was turned around to look back. "... Aaron ..." who just smiled. "... I'm Mark, and that's Jay ..." who saluted. "... And this little guy is Caleb."

"Hi," Caleb said in a mini voice.

"Well, I sure do appreciate you guys saving me like that. I feel like it's every person for themselves right now; at least that's how I felt when a few people just ran away from me and said they weren't gonna help me."

"You're not bit or scratched or anything, are you?" I asked looking in the rearview again.

"No, I think it's 'cause they didn't know who I was."

"Well, I hate to interrupt the get to know one another session, but we are about to come up on N&P and it looks like a lot of people had the same idea we did, there are tons of zombies out here. Gonna be more inside. What should I do, Jay?"

"Drive up to the front doors and park the van in front of the glass window. That way they won't see us walking around in there and start hording in front of the window. We'll clear out what we have to go get inside, and then we'll just make some noise and have the zombies inside come to us. That way we can shoot them without us getting hurt."

"Sounds like a plan," Mark said as he dug in his duffle bag and pulled out ammo and a gun for Carron. "Lock and load, everyone." He passed around new clips for everybody, and we all got ready to jump out and shoot to get inside the store. When we jumped out we started shooting at any that were close enough to cause a problem and ran for the door; we just weren't banking on the front door being locked. "Why the hell is it locked?"

"Around the side!" shouted Jay.

Everyone went running around the side and stopped short as there were about six zombies lingering in the alleyway by the door. Bullets flew and zombies went down. Next thing we knew, the door was coming open and this little old lady was standing there, "Hurry up and get inside!" Everyone ran past her, and she shut and locked the door behind them.

Once inside, everyone caught their breath and was looking at the old lady. Jay was still hunched over but managed to breathe, "Thanks, Ma." Two seconds later she was hugging him so tight. "Too tight, Ma, too tight!"

"Oh, sorry, Jay dear. I'm just so glad to see you. I told that old coot you wouldn't abandon us."

"Where is Joe?"

"He's over here, but you got to be quiet; there are still some zombies up front and we've been back here hiding."

They walked to the other end of the store room behind the actual store to the office where Jay's step-dad Joe was sitting with his head on the desk.

"Joe, look who's here."

Joe looked up and didn't look well at all. He was a light ashen color and was sweating profusely. "Hiya, my boy."

WINTER OF THE HUNGRY

"Joe, you don't look so well." Then Jay noticed the blood on the side of his stomach. "Were you bit?" He bent down to look and lifted his shirt and saw the bloodied gauze soaked through. Looking back at the others, "Will you guys go clear out the store and see what you can find for food? And be careful."

"No problem," said Mark as he turned the others toward the store door. "Carron, will you stay here with Caleb?"

"Sure; hey, Caleb, wanna see a trick?

"Ya!" he said excitedly as she walked him back to a few crates and sat down.

"Oh, I'm gonna have to change that again. I don't know why just a scratch is bleeding so much." Jay's mom shook her head as she grabbed a new piece of gauze, some tape, and alcohol pads.

"Mom, who scratched him?"

"Oh, stupid snobby Ms. Perloyto, that one that thinks she's better than everyone because she gets to live off her husband's social security and walks around like she owns everything. She tried to bite him, of all things, while we were shopping. I pushed her off of him and we ran back here, and she must have scratched him when I pushed her. I'd like to punch the old broad."

"Mom, if you get scratched or bit by a zombie, you turn." Jay looked at Joe. "You will turn."

"I know, my boy, but your mother is stubborn and wanted me to stay with her until you got here, felt you were the way to fix it."

"Mom, there's no way to fix it. It's permanent."

His mom was too busy changing the dressing, and seemed to not hear a single word. "Where's Ann?"

"She's dead, Mom; she didn't make it."

Jay's mom finally stopped and reality started to sink in. "Dead?" Tears started to appear and then a great sobbing started. "What nightmare are we in? Why is this happening to us?"

Jay hugged her, "I don't know Mom, I don't know."

WINTER OF THE HUNGRY

Looking at his step-dad over her shoulder, he could tell Joe knew he didn't have much time left.

Just then there was a bunch of noise coming from the front of the shop. Jay got up and ran into the store to help. There was one old lady zombie trying to bite me and everyone was trying to shoot her but they were afraid of hitting me.

"Shoot her already, dammit!" I shouted at them.

Jay knew they couldn't because I'd be hit too and was trying to find something to hit her in the head with, when his mother came out of nowhere, swinging a broom and yelling, "You snobby ole' coot! I'm gonna kill you for what you did to my Joe!" She swung the broomstick and hit Ms. Perloyto upside the head with it, and when she turned around she growled at her and Jay's mom jammed the broomstick right throw her mouth out the back of her head. "Take that, you stiff-necked fossilized bitch!"

"Thanks, Jay's mom," I said as I looked down at the now dead zombified Ms. Perloyto.

WINTER OF THE HUNGRY

"The name's Ruth."

"Your mom's a badass, Jay," snickered Josh.

"Now where do you think he got his attitude from?" winked Ruth.

Ruth was a cop's daughter, which is one of the reasons why Jay wanted to work in security. She was raised a tomboy, knowing how to take care of herself and how to fight because her father wanted her to know that sometimes there is nobody there to protect you but yourself and he didn't want to see his daughter on a slab because she couldn't fight for herself. Ruth never wanted to work in job that was so full of violence so she decided just to be a mom. It was one of the greatest jobs she could have ever held and she was paid in kisses. However, before she was able to fulfill that dream she had to find a job to pay for living expenses, so she decided to try a hand at modeling. Ruth was a very beautiful woman in her younger years and could turn heads from miles away. She had black hair and flawless skin with beautiful green eyes. She was very photogenic and one of her pictures even made it into a magazine. Her father was not very happy with her but her picture made her even more popular with men and thus she ended up getting her dream of being a mom. Jay's father did not stick around but then she met Joe and Ruth got her dream life and was happy with the way it ended up.

Jay and Ruth went back to the backroom while everyone else started packing food supplies in their backpacks. Caleb and Carron came up to help after Aaron had taken some of the table cloths and covered up the file of zombies they had stacked in a corner. Once all the commotion was over, they heard the speakers in the store still playing Christmas music, and it made the mood in the room lighten up a little bit. The people forgot for just a second what was going on on their little island.

"What are we gonna do now?" asked Ruth, looking at her son.

"Well, we could head over to the hospital and see if there

are some antibiotics, and stitch this up to help stop the bleeding.

"You'd only be delaying the inevitable, my boy."

"I know that, but I'm not ready to lose you yet, do you hear me?" Ruth said with a sob her throat. "We at least have to try."

"Well, then it's settled. We will pack what we can into our bags and head for the hospital. It's probably gonna be crawling with zombies, so we have to be careful. The pharmacy is on the first floor down the hall, and if I remember right, there is a small surgical room at the end of the same hall, so we shouldn't have to go any farther than that."

Josh and I came back into the room and heard the last part of the conversation. "Look, I know that your step-dad is sick, but we need to rest. We aren't gonna be no help to anyone, especially ourselves, if we are so tired we can't think straight. Can he make it until morning? It's too dark out there to see what's out there anyway. We wouldn't be safe," I pointed out.

"Ya, you're right but I don't think he has until morning.

WINTER OF THE HUNGRY

I'll run over there myself and grab the stuff; that way it's in and out, and then I'll come back," Jay suggested.

Aaron interrupted, "I'm coming with you. You are not doing it alone. You need back up."

"All right then, it's settled. Mom, I'll be right back, I promise. Hang on, Joe." As Jay looked from his mom to his step-dad, he turned toward Aaron. "You got ammo?"

"Yup, I'm good."

Mark suggested they take one of the walkies just in case, "You never know if you might need backup or if something changes here and the store is compromised."

"Thanks." Jay took the walkie from Mark and put it on his belt clip. They slowly opened the side door and saw only a few zombies at the end of the alley shining under the street lights.

"We'll be back as soon as we can," Jay said as he shut the door behind him. Looking at Aaron, he said, "Only shoot if you need to; we need to save our bullets just in case. It might be very populated in the hospital."

"Okay."

Aaron and Jay snuck down the alley in the dark which provided the perfect cover, not only for them, but also for the zombies; luckily, there weren't any sneaking in the dark at that time. At the end of the alley were just a few that were wandering down the street passing by the alley like it wasn't even there. The hospital was on the next block over. If they could cross the street without being detected, they could run down the next alley and then cross the street, again undetected, to get to the front door. Easy.

Looking both ways before crossing the street, they saw only a few zombies here and there. Seemed they all kind of meandered away from the grocery store. Jay looked back at Aaron and whispered, "Let's go," and pointed to the next alley.

They both took off running and were seen by one zombie, but he was moving too slowly and was about a half a block down, so he didn't pose a threat. They got to the alley safe and sound, again covered by the protection of the dark. However, they could hear something moving around in the dark with them but just didn't know where. Jay whispered again, "Be careful," to Aaron as they lurked down the alley.

"MEEEOOOWWW!" screamed a cat, as Jay stepped on its tail and it went running down the alley.

"Whoops," Jay said chuckling to himself. "At least we know what the noise was now," he said in a whisper. However, that cat not only had its poor tail stepped on, but its scream was also like an alarm letting all zombies in the area know that there was something going on in that alley that they just had to check out.

The end of the alley emptied onto the drive up route for the ambulance, so this wasn't a thoroughfare for pedestrians. There was an ambulance sitting there half up on the curb with its lights flashing and the driver's side door hanging open. As Jay and

WINTER OF THE HUNGRY

Aaron slowly walked up to it, they heard noises coming from around the back. As Jay had his weapon at the ready, he slowly slid down the side of the ambulance and peeked around the corner. One of the back doors was open, but the one closest to Jay was still closed. Jay slowly looked through the window of the door and saw the EMT driver eating what was left of the patient he had been transporting. Jay leaned over just enough to take aim and shot the EMT in the head.

Jay turned back to look at Aaron, "Let's get in and out as quickly and as quietly as possible."

Nodding his head in agreement, Aaron and Jay headed into the hospital to get the supplies that were needed to save Joe, but were unaware of the dangers that lurked within and the ones that were now gathering behind them, blocking their means of escape.

Chapter 12

WINTER OF THE HUNGRY

"I hope they got over there and inside okay." Worrying about her son, Ruth wondered if his mental state was okay after just losing the love of his life. Mark filled her in on what had happened and she knew that it was the only way, but her baby must be hurting so badly because of it. After this was all said and done, she would make sure that Ann had a proper burial and funeral service. She deserved it. Ann had made Jay so happy and Ruth too.

When Jay proposed, Ruth might have been a little happier than Ann had been. She had always wanted a daughter, but Jay was the only child that God had granted her, and now she finally had that chance. The wedding was beautiful; Jay and Ann had gotten married in the field next to Ruth's home and the day had been so lovely. Everything was perfect, and everyone had been happy. Now, there was nothing but sadness, and Ruth didn't know if Jay would actually be able to function once the rush of adrenaline quieted down when they finally got off the island. Ann

WINTER OF THE HUNGRY

was his rock. Ruth just hoped that Jay kept fighting until they all were safe.

She looked over at Joe. "You okay, honey?"

"Ya, just really tired. I'm just gonna close my eyes a bit, okay, dear?"

"Sure thing, I'll just go out into the store with the others and give you some quiet time." She kissed Joe on the head and watched her husband put his head down on the desk as she pulled the door closed, knowing that she too would soon be alone in this life without a person to share it with.

As Ruth walked through the storage room, she could hear a lot of deep breathing mixed in with the still playing Christmas music but also, someone's snorting snores. She looked over and found the source of the sound: Josh. Each of the members of the group had dozed off, if only for a few minutes here and there, but Josh was completely out cold.

I was always a light sleeper and opened my eyes as Ruth

had come in and watched her stop and stare at Josh. "He could be in the middle of a tornado and would still sleep like that. I don't know how he does it."

"Ya, well that's great and all, but he needs to not get any louder or it might attract more zombies our way."

I got up and walked over to Josh, "Josh, psst Josh." Shaking him. "Wake up, dude, you're snoring too loud."

Josh opened his eyes in a panic, "What the hell, dude? Kary Sanders was about to take her shirt off!"

"You are such a dork."

"Who's Kary Sanders?" asked Ruth

"Oh, she's this actress that has the same birthday as Josh, and he thinks she's so hot."

"She's more than just hot, Itchy, she's a God. Aw, man! That sucks." He shook his head, and rubbed his face. "Hey, did you ever think that if this, whatever this is, gets off the island that all the sexy people would become zombies? That would really blow."

"Ya, you would have to find old Bunny Hunny magazines or something to spank off to."

"Oh, shut up, man!"

Ruth piped in, "Just stay away from June 1980 issue, or you might never look at me the same way again." She winked at me and Josh as she turned and sat down on a chair in the corner to catch a little nap.

Josh and I just looked at each other and started snickering before lying back down on the floor to try and catch some more sleep.

Across the street in the hospital ...

"Seriously? Even the hospital is playing Christmas music? I don't know if I can take much more of this," Aaron complained.

"Ya, I'm not feeling especially jolly at the moment either. Betcha there's a way to shut it off behind one of the main desks, but it could also mask any noise we make so we don't attract zombies our way. We might wanna leave it on."

"True that." Sneaking through the hallways, they were surprised at how clear they were. They had expected, coming from any zombie movie out there, that the hospital would be crawling with zombies. "Guess they all walked out already," Aaron suggested.

"Guess so; let's just get the gauze and get out of here. I don't wanna have to go any further in than necessary." They headed toward the pharmacy, slowly checking each of the doors before continuing so that there was nothing that was going to keep them from returning the way they had come. One door was closed. "Let's just leave it shut, saves on noise, and bullets," Jay said as he and Aaron walked past it.

There was no warning upon coming up to the next door when out walked a nurse in purple scrubs with the nametag Vicki N. etched on it. She had a needle sticking out of her eye and she reached out and grabbed Jay and was trying to bite him as he continuously tried to push her away. They were dancing in circles as she pushed him up against the wall, being much stronger than he anticipated and as she was leaning in, he could see that she had a bite on her neck. He thought to himself that this was the way his life was going to end, and he would be with Ann again. Slowly he lost focus on the bite mark and raised his gaze to what was behind Vicki N., it was Aaron saying, "Duck!"

Jay ducked and slid to the floor. Aaron took a run at Vicki N., and the needle casing hit the wall and shoved all the way into her head and she fell to the floor in a lump next to Jay.

"Thanks," Jay said as he reached up for the hand Aaron offered.

"Don't thank me yet; we gotta move!"

Jay looked around Aaron and saw that the commotion had stirred the zombies in the area and they were coming for lunch. The two ran down the hallway, not even checking the doors and dove over the counter into the pharmacy.

WINTER OF THE HUNGRY

"You find the antibiotics and I'll run over to the surgery room and get the surgical equipment we need. Stay sharp, and be quick!" Jay said as he ran around the corner of the counter and through the swinging doors of the surgical room. Aaron ran into the shelving and started looking for penicillin, because that was the only antibiotic that he knew about.

Jay saw that one zombie was still lying on the operating table but was strapped down with a neck brace on. Must have come in from an accident, he was trying to get free to get at Jay as he walked around the room. There was another body in the corner of the room but it wasn't moving and Jay didn't want to waste the time to check it. He just wanted to get in and out as fast as possible. He grabbed one of the shelving units and started dumping stuff into his bag, not realizing that with his back away from the body in the corner he didn't see it get up off the floor and start moving towards him.

Jay turned around to grab some of the other items off the

table next to the gurney, "Holy shit!" he shouted as the doctor that was the body in the corner was suddenly in his face. The doctor had surgical gloves and a mask on but the mask was missing a chunk and so was the face underneath it as if someone had given him a fatal kiss.

All of a sudden the doc's brains splattered all over the wall and on Jay's head as Aaron had come in the door and shot the dead doc in the head. "We gotta go!" shouted Aaron as he held the door open for Jay. They ran into the hall and saw that the crew of zombies was getting too close for comfort. They started shooting the closest ones, then ran around the corner and saw that there were more zombies heading in from the back hallway. Jay and Aaron's only exit was into the stairwell.

Running into the stairwell, they could hear the zombies that were stuck in there with them due to the great acoustics, which also means they could hear Jay and Aaron.

"We gotta get out of here. If we go up to the second level

WINTER OF THE HUNGRY

we can jump out a window and make it to the street without injury," suggested Jay as he started up the stairs with Aaron in tow. However, with the slamming of the door, the stairwell zombies were already headed in their direction. Considering they were coming down, some didn't have the best balance because of missing limbs or broken bones and started falling right in front of them and the door to the second level. "Shit. Just start shooting!"

Shooting the zombies that were trying to grab them and stepping over the ones that didn't pose that much of a threat, they ended up using a lot of ammo trying to get to the second level doorway. One of the ones on the floor grabbed Aaron's ankle and he aimed down and shot it just before it bit him and then continued shooting the ones between them and the door.

What they didn't realize is that the door had a key card entry and when they got to it, there was a whole herd of zombies coming from above and below them.

"Damn!" yelled Jay as he saw the card reader.

WINTER OF THE HUNGRY

Aaron looked around and noticed that one of the zombies heading toward them had a badge. He was an Asian in scrubs and a doctor's coat and the name on the badge was Dr. Robert Ryoo M.D., F.A.C.C., and the word Cardiology under his name. He grabbed it as Dr. Ryoo tried grabbing for him and pulled the retractable string and slid the card through. The light on the card reader turned green, and then Aaron pushed Dr. Ryoo down the stairs. He and Jay walked through the door and fought with a few zombies' arms in the way of shutting the door.

"Just pull it! Break the arms off if you have to!" Jay yelled as they struggled to shut the door. A few fingers and a hand got cut off, but they managed to get the door shut. Standing back, they watched the zombie faces smash themselves against the window as they tried to get through.

"We need to get to a window and get out of here." Aaron didn't like hospitals, especially this floor. It was the surgery floor and this is where he spent a lot of time as a child. His father was

Winter of the Hungry

born in the United Kingdom and had a lot of health issues. Due to that, he needed a lot of surgeries and his grandparents had decided to come to America for the medical breakthroughs.

Aaron's mother told him that they mostly had to remove and fix different insides that were broken when they were at the hospital. They spent so much time at the hospital between the surgeries and the recovery time that they were probably there more than they were at home. Aaron didn't understand at the time because he was too young but his father had a congenital heart defect and cystic fibrosis. Aaron never showed any signs of inheriting it.

His father didn't have much time left at that point that Aaron could remember. Aaron was only five when his father finally passed away, his father was 24. Aaron since associated his father's death with the hospital and has hated it ever since.

"Let's get into the nearest room on the south side that faces N&P and we'll get out of here," Jay suggested.

WINTER OF THE HUNGRY

They ran to the nearest room and looked out the window. Mark's voice came over the walkie at that point. "Guys, you're gonna have to find a different route out of the hospital. There's a horde gathering in the alleyway."

"Yup, we just noticed." As Jay looked out he could see that the noise he had made by stepping on the cat had attracted a ton of zombies and they were blocking the alley completely. "We may just have to go out the other side and sneak around the building," Jay said into the walkie.

"10-4. Hurry up, Jay, I don't think your dad has much time left, and your mom's getting worried."

"Got it. Be there as fast as we can." Looking at Aaron, he said, "Let's get out of here before it gets worse out there."

"No doubt."

They had made so much noise with the door that the zombies on second level had meandered in their direction and were blocking sections of the hallway.

WINTER OF THE HUNGRY

"Crap, we can't get out."

"Can we go out the window and hop onto the fire escape of the next building?" Aaron asked.

Jay looked out and saw that the fire escape for the hospital window and the one for the next building weren't all that far away. The only problem was that the hospital window had a safety latch on it so patients couldn't just open the window and get out. The safety latch was a key card reader like the one on the stairwell door.

Aaron stuck his hands in his pockets. "Um, I didn't realize it until just now, but when I grabbed that key card from the zombie, it snapped off his pull string and I accidentally stuck it in my pocket while we were trying to shut the door."

"Well, isn't that lucky?"

Aaron swiped the card and they opened the window and climbed out onto the fire escape. The zombies below were oblivious to their presence, but that wouldn't be the case for much longer. They climbed out over the railing. "I'll jump first and then when you jump, I'll make sure I catch you."

"Okay," Agreed Aaron. "Just make sure you don't drop me."

After some self-convincing, Jay took at leap across the space between the fire escapes and barely made it. Once on the other side, he had some worry that Aaron wouldn't be able to make the jump. "Take the biggest leap you can, it's wider than it looks."

"Gotcha." Aaron's build made him the worst candidate for jumping. He was a weight lifter, not a hurdler. Counting under his breath to himself, "1 ... 2 ... 3!" On three he jumped, but did not get enough oomph to get to the railing or reach Jay's outstretched hand. As he fell, he thought about Scarlett and knew this was payback for how he had treated her. He didn't have time to think much else as he fell into the wire awning that covered the building's back door which snapped his spine, and he fell to the ground not being able to feel the zombies tear him apart piece by piece. The last thing he did before he died as blood was coming from his mouth was mouth the word, "Scarlett."

Jay shook his head and wiped it with his hand. He didn't know what he was going to do if he kept losing people. He had to be focused, though; he was in an abandoned apartment complex that was being renovated and was supposed to be attached to the hospital by a sky walk. However, planning had stalled because of asbestos and the contractor was waiting on a tester to come out and see if it was safe to restart construction. There should be nobody in this building so it should've been easy to walk right out the front door. At least that's what Jay hoped.

It seems that a lot of the people had the same idea when they were in the streets running away from zombies, and that was to hide in the abandoned building. However, some of those people had been bit or scratched and turned while inside. The ones that had run inside to hide from the zombies that had not been bit or scratched weren't any more safe on the inside than they were on the outside. There may have been only a few zombies here or there throughout the building, due to one person getting attacked by the front door so the blood smeared on it deterred would be victims away after that point, but there was still enough to pose a threat to Jay and his ability to get back to the N&P safely.

Talking to himself, he said, "I have to make it back, if I lose one more person ..." Which wasn't necessarily a good idea when he shouldn't be making noise or attracting attention to himself. Granted, he wasn't being loud, but if any of them heard him, he'd make his odds of getting out alive a lot more difficult. "This is ridiculous. This is not some horror movie; I have to be dreaming here. Zombies! Really?" He continued mumbling to himself and making his way through the hallways to the stairs because he was pretty sure that the elevator wouldn't be a safe way to go even if the power was on. "I lost Ann, I lost my dear dear Ann; how could this really be happening? All those movies show this going on forever, never ending; is this how life is gonna be

WINTER OF THE HUNGRY

now? A never ending zombie movie?" All of a sudden, there was this noise that snapped Jay back to notice what was going on around him. "What the hell was that?" It sounded like a whimper of some sort, like an animal or something. Jay stopped and listened and heard it again. It was coming from behind the door of room 213. He listened at the door and could hear the whimpering, "Sounds like a dog," Jay said to himself. Building courage to open the door and also making sure he had ammo in his gun, he held the pistol up head high and slowly opened the door. He didn't even get it open all the way when out ran a short Greyhound type dog which scared Jay and knocked him to the floor. "What the ...?" Jay, who had dropped his gun when he fell to the floor, was looking at the dog and didn't notice the owner of the dog come barreling through the door, zombified.

"BARK!" The dog warned Jay at the impending danger.

Jay looked up. "Holy Shit!" He rolled over to where he saw his gun had gone and as the zombie came towards him and was about to land on him, he shot her straight in the middle of the head, and she still ended up landing on him but at least she was already dead, or rather dead again.

"Whimper whimper ..." The dog walked up to the lady that Jay just shot and pushed at her hand with its nose, then laid down on the floor and just stared at her.

"Was that your owner there, little fella?"

The dog just wagged its tail.

"Come here, puppy."

The dog got up and slowly walked over to Jay and tucked its tail between its legs and bowed its head down in fear.

"I won't hurt ya, just wanna see what your name is." Checking the tag, the name on it said NIKKI and underneath was an address and the words OWNER and JOSLYNN. "Is your name Nikki?"

Nikki wagged her tail and stuck her tongue out and panted for a few seconds.

WINTER OF THE HUNGRY

"Well, pardon me for calling you a fella earlier," he said, as he scratched behind her head. "Nikki, let's get some food into you because I'm sure you are hungry; it's only proper since you did save my life. But first we hafta get out of here, and the noise I made is not gonna help us." As Jay walked down the hallway, he turned around and saw that Nikki was still standing next to Joslynn. "Come on, girl," he called as he patted his leg.

Nikki whimpered again and looked back and forth between Joslynn and Jay and then ran down the hallway towards Jay.

Meanwhile at the N&P ...

"I wonder what's taking Jay and Aaron so long? I hope they are all right." Ruth wondered to herself; she was worried. She didn't want to lose anyone else. She already lost a wonderful daughter-in-law and her husband was very ill and probably not going to make it; she couldn't fathom losing Jay too. All of a sudden there was a noise in the office where Joe was. Ruth got up from her chair and ran over to the office door. Josh stopped her.

WINTER OF THE HUNGRY

"What's in there may not be your husband anymore. Let me. Itchy?"

"Right behind you."

Josh opened the door and saw that Joe had fallen off the chair and onto the floor. Josh and I slowly walked over. Josh checked his pulse while I kept a gun on him. Josh looked at me and then to Ruth. "I'm sorry, Ruth, there's no pulse."

"No!" she sobbed as she walked over to coddle her husband but in that moment the body started to move, Josh jumped back, I waited only a split second for Joe's eyes to open and know for sure that he was a zombie before I shot him. Of course, I had closed my eyes and missed the forehead by about three inches or so and shot him in the nose which made a mess. Ruth ran from the room and into Carron's arms who was standing around the corner with Caleb. Ruth leaned back and looked at Mark, "I need Jay to come back safe, I need him to; he's all I have left."

The noise from the shot, however, attracted some zombies

WINTER OF THE HUNGRY

who were now banging on the back door and a couple were starting to gather up front by the windows. "If enough of them start banging on the glass, we might have a real problem. We need to move out, it's no longer safe. I'll radio Jay and see if he's okay. Jay? Come in, Jay, store's no longer safe; need to move, what's your ETA?"

There was no answer, Aaron had the walkie when he fell which, with Mark's voice coming through, even though it was a little broken up because of the fall, still attracted the zombies more toward the middle of the driveway between the hotel and the hospital, and the echo actually kept the other zombies from moving towards the store.

"We gotta move before there are too many. If we quietly kill the ones in front of the glass we can get into the truck and drive towards the boat launch," urged Mark.

"But what about Jay? I'm not leaving him behind." Ruth intently stared at Mark.

WINTER OF THE HUNGRY

"I'm sorry, Ruth, but in reality if he's not answering, he's either somewhere where he can't answer or he's already dead."

Ruth gasped.

"I'm sorry, Ruth, but we have to admit it."

Caleb interrupted, "Can't we leave him a note like we did with my mom?"

"Great idea, little man," Josh said as he patted him on the head. "Let's find one of those window writing things, they gotta have one here somewhere right? To write on the window for sales and stuff?"

"Ya, I'll help you look, it's probably in the office, so let me go in there," I offered.

The poor lady, I thought to myself as I stepped over Joe's body. I rummaged through the drawers and found some white glass chalk. I walked out to the store area, "Found some!"

Ruth walked over as I handed it to her and walked up to the window, "We're going to the boat launch, right?"

WINTER OF THE HUNGRY

"That's the plan," Josh answered.

"Okay, then that's what I'm putting on the window. GONE TO BOAT LAUNCH -WASN'T SAFE, LOVE, MOM." Ruth read out loud as she wrote backwards on the window so Jay could read it without having to come in. "That was a great idea, Caleb dear, thank you." She knelt down and hugged him.

"Okay, it's getting colder out, and we don't know if the next place we will be will have heat so bundle up and get all the bags together; there will be no coming back for anything. As soon as that truck starts the zombies are gonna swarm." Mark wanted to make sure everyone got in that truck safely. "I'm gonna go out and stab these two in the head; will you watch my back for any others?" He looked at Josh.

"Yup, I got your 6."

Mark opened the door and while I kept the zombies occupied at the other end of the wall, he stepped out and got the first one, no problem, but the knife got a little stuck and without having another arm to push the zombie off his knife he was gonna be in trouble really quickly. As he struggled to get his knife loose, Josh stepped past him and got the other one just as it was getting too close for comfort. Mark got his knife finally loose and in one move side swung his arm into the head of the third one, whispering, "Okay, guys, let's move." Opening the passenger door of the truck, they all started filing inside and moving to the back; Ruth first, then Caleb and Carron, and then the guys.

The back doors of the truck were still open, and while Mark started the truck, Josh and I pulled the doors closed, but my side, because of the small incline in the truck was on, had swung open so far that it locked itself in the open position. I jumped out as zombies were starting to come forward because of the noise. "I gotta get this door unlocked from the side of the truck!"

Josh shot a few zombies that were getting too close and yelled at me, "Hurry up!"

"I am! Just start moving, and I'll do it as we go so we can

stay ahead of them."

"I heard that." Mark put the truck into gear and slowing started inching forward as I kept messing with the latch.

I finally got it loose, "Let's move!"

Mark hit the gas.

As I swung the door and went to jump into the truck I heard something.

"BARK!"

I looked behind me after I jumped on the truck and saw a dog running and behind the dog was Jay. "Jay! It's Jay! And a dog!"

Mark slowed down enough and the dog, being part Greyhound, had no problem catching the truck. Josh and I helped it inside and then helped Jay as he jumped aboard. Ruth ran over and hugged Jay. She spun him around so her back was to the door which was still open. "We lost Joe, honey," she said with a sniff. All of a sudden, the truck shook and looking at the open door there

WINTER OF THE HUNGRY

was a huge man dressed as a clown climbing into the truck and grabbing at Ruth. He got hold of her leg and pulled her backward out the door and was already biting her by the time the Jay realized what had happened. Josh shot the clown but there were other zombies coming up fast and there was no time to save Ruth. Even if there was, it was impossible to save someone with a zombie bite. She was doomed.

She knew there was no other choice, "I love you, honey!" shouted Ruth. Jay held out his gun and shot her in head.

"Someone shut that Goddamn door!" shouted Mark from the driver's seat.

Jay slumped over in the back of the van and mumbled to himself, "I love you too, Mom," as I shut and latched the door closed.

Carron and Caleb had moved to the passenger seat before the dog and Jay jumped on, and Mark looked over at her, rolled his eyes, and stated, "I fucking hate clowns."

CHAPTER 13

WINTER OF THE HUNGRY

Nobody said a word. Not because they didn't want to, but we just didn't know what exactly we should say. We had all lost people over the last 24 hours but this poor man, lost his wife, step-father, and mother all within a few short hours and he had to kill two of them himself. I was the first to speak.

"Jay? What happened to Aaron?" Not that it was better subject to bring up, but even though I didn't really like the guy, I felt the need to know.

"When Mark called over the radio and told us that the zombies were crowding the front door, we actually got pushed up to the second level and had to jump from the balcony onto the one on the old hotel. I jumped first but when Aaron jumped ... he just didn't jump far enough. I think he actually broke something on the fall though because he didn't scream or anything while ... well ... you know."

"Oh, how terrible!" exclaimed Carron.

"Where'd you find the dog?" Josh asked as he ruffled

WINTER OF THE HUNGRY

Nikki's ears and played with her.

"I was walking down a hallway and heard some noise which happened to be her whimpering in one of the rooms. I think her owner and her had been hiding but not before her owner was scratched or bit. I fell when I opened the door and didn't notice the owner come out of the room because I was looking at the dog. Nikki actually barked and warned me. I got my gun and shot the owner right before she would have got me." At the mention of her name Nikki ran over to Jay and put her front paws on him. "Isn't that right, girl?"

I thought to myself that at least the conversation I'd taken, got Jay's mind off of his loss for at least a little bit. All of a sudden the truck slowed down fast.

"Ah, what's going on?" Josh said, getting up and looking out the front.

Mark answered, "Look for yourself." We all got up and looked out the windshield and saw under the street lights of the dock that pretty much everyone else that had survived had the same idea they did and had gone straight for the docks to take their boats off the island. However, because some were infected or had been bit, the zombification spread throughout everyone that was at the pier and now the whole place was filled with zombie town people. It didn't look like there was going to be a way to get through and still survive.

"Oh, my God," exclaimed Josh. "Now, what the hell we gonna do?"

"Not sure."

"Can't we use some of your grenades and blast them all?" I asked Mark.

"No. The dock was made so long ago that even one could blast it apart and the waves from the bits and pieces and bodies landing in the water will push the boats farther out, making it more difficult to get to them."

"Okay, I have an idea," interrupted Jay. "There's a private

boat launch for the governmental facility actually behind it. The only way to get to it is to have an access badge that allows you to scan in on an exiting hallway on the other side of the warehouse."

"That's all fine and dandy but we don't have badges and I don't feel like wrestling a zombie for theirs. Plus, what's to say that that dock isn't loaded too?" I asked.

"Well, the only people with badges are the sergeants and any top ranking government employee, and they don't work during holiday breaks so they wouldn't have been here to open the door for anyone."

Everyone lowered their heads, Josh rolled his eyes, and Caleb admitted to Carron, "I'm scared."

"I know, dear; we all are," she answered back as she hugged him.

"Well, there goes that idea," Josh stated as he stomped into the back of the truck and sat down.

"Well, there is one other person that has access to that

hallway," Jay grinned.

"Who?" we all asked in unison.

"Me." Jay pulled his badge out of his shirt pocket. "I have to check that hallway on rounds every day to make sure no unauthorized people are illegally using the dock."

"You snot!" yelled Carron. "You were scaring Caleb!"

"Sorry, I didn't mean to, little buddy."

Caleb sniffed and wiped some snot from his face on his shirt, "That's okay. Are we gonna be safe then?"

"Well, biggest problem is getting past all the other facility staff. They may have been turned, but if not and they are holed up inside, they won't let just anyone waltz through a government facility without authority."

"I'd hate to interrupt, but we better decide fast what we are doing because that group that was at the store is catching up to us the longer we sit here." Josh pointed out the back door window as he looked at the horde of zombies headed their way from the streets of town. Carron also commented, "The townsfolk in front of us at the docks are starting to notice and move this way too."

"Okay, sounds like a plan; we can talk and drive and decide what to do when we get there." Mark threw the truck into gear and stalled. "Are you fucking kidding me? Now?!" Mark tried again and all it did was whirr. "Oh please, if you are up there, start the fucking truck!" Mark was not a religious person but at this point he'd try anything. He turned it again and it revved to life. "Guess I need to go back to church when this is over," he chuckled and had to turn around to get back to the road for the facility. He slid a little bit as he turned on the newly fallen snow but he got control and barely made it as the horde came inches from the bumper. He took off down the road to the facility, leaving the zombies behind, for now.

"So how we gonna do this?" asked Mark, as he drove the curvy 2.5 mile road down to the facility.

"Well, there's a gate and a guard booth; if there is any kind of explosion, the guard is supposed to lock the gate and report to the other side of the plant to assist with rescue personnel coming on site to help. So the gate will either be locked and if not surrounded by zombies I can unlock it with my key, or it will be unlocked and I suggest driving right through. I'll tell you where to go from there."

"Sounds good."

The passenger side windshield wiper got stuck and Carron opened her window to try and push it to move again, which distracted Mark from the road and he didn't see the really sharp corner before the gate. The guard shack came into view, and because Mark was only half paying attention, he took the corner a little faster than he should have and lost control of the truck. "Hold on!"

The group fell over each other as the truck started to flip onto its side. Josh fell towards the back as the door popped open and he fell out. Carron lost her grip on Caleb, and he fell out the passenger window as the truck finally landed. Nikki yipped as she rolled and stumbled in the back of the truck. I fell into Jay and we rolled onto our backs as the truck slid on down the snowy road. Mark had his seatbelt on and just hung in his seat until the truck finally came to a stop.

Josh got up from where he had fallen and rolled and looked around and saw the aftermath of what happened to Caleb. He ran to the truck and could hear Carron screaming; she had climbed over Mark to climb out the driver's window calling Caleb's name. "Caleb? Caleb? Where are you? I'm coming!"

Josh scrambled to get to the top of the door before she saw, and grabbed her as she came out and turned her back towards the remains. "He's gone, Carron, he's gone. Don't look; you don't wanna see that."

He hugged her as she screamed and sobbed, "No!"

"Itchy? Itchy you okay? Jay?" Josh could see Mark from where he was standing and could see he was okay.

WINTER OF THE HUNGRY

Mark turned his head around and unbuckled his seatbelt, falling to the passenger seat. "Oof, I'll look." He climbed over the seat and got to me and Jay. We were both knocked out cold. "They're breathing just knocked out. The dog's okay, I think; she's whining."

"Well, they better wake up fast! That noise made a lot of close zombies curious, and the horde is catching up; we gotta move."

"I got some smelling salts in my bag, but I don't know where it went." Mark looked around and realized it had fallen off the truck when the door opened. He crawled out and looked around. Mark wished he had a flashlight. The bag was black and because of how dark it was, he couldn't see where it had landed. He walked along the side of the road and eventually saw it in the ditch. Running over and sliding in the snow, he grabbed it and saw what Josh was so desperately trying to conceal from Carron. It was not a pretty sight. Even though all he could really see were the streaks of blood in the snow from the taillights, it was still not something that he would want to describe to anyone, ever. He grabbed the bag and ran and slid back over to the truck. After climbing back inside, he unzipped the bag and dug around for the salts.

"Hurry up, Mark we're running out of time." It was so dark that Josh couldn't see exactly where the zombies were, but he could hear them and he kept looking over his shoulder and to the left and right to make sure none snuck up on them. He didn't like the dark, especially in this case.

Jay started to come around on his own, and snapped up. "Everyone okay?" He moved over to Nikki, who had stopped whining.

"I think she was only scared, but we lost Caleb," Mark answered as he finally found the salts and broke one under my nose.

I moved my head some and moaned. "What the heck?

WINTER OF THE HUNGRY

Ow, my head." I stated as I reached up to rub it.

"No time to tend to wounds; can't see them anyway. We gotta get out of here; the zombies are coming and we can't see them."

Josh had to quiet Carron who was mumbling about Caleb. "He was just a kid; he didn't deserve that."

"Ssh, Carron, we have to listen so we can survive now, okay?"

"'K."

There was no lighting on this particular road like there was through the streets of town, and the five of us remaining survivors and our dog had to blindly walk down a road with only the lights from the truck to light their way. Only one of us had ever been down this road and we hoped that what went bump in the night didn't find us. We could see the gate at the end, and it was closed. We wouldn't be able to tell if it was locked until we got closer but because of the night and the cold, it was becoming unbearable just

WINTER OF THE HUNGRY

walking that short distance. It may have been only 200 feet or so, but it felt like miles in that cold whipping wind and snow. Nikki's feet started to get so cold she couldn't walk anymore and Jay had to carry her.

"I hope we g ... g ... get there s ... s ... soon," Josh stammered as his teeth chattered together. Because of the snow and the wind they couldn't even see the lights of the facility, unless of course they aren't even on and that was the reason they couldn't see them.

"We have to k ... k ... keep going. It's not m ... m ... much farther. Achoo!" Jay managed to get out before he sneezed, almost losing his balance because of Nikki.

Just then a light started to faintly come into view. "Th ... there it is!" pointed Carron.

We all looked up and saw the faint light of hope and heat in the closing distance. Zombies or not, we just wanted to get inside. Then we all picked up the pace a bit and got to the gate in no time, but it was locked. Jay reached for his keys and, handing Nikki off to Mark, began trying to unlock the frozen lock. Having to breathe on the lock and the key a few times to get it to function, he finally got it unlocked. Not only did he have to unlock a padlock but also had to punch in a pin code to access the gate's automatic opening mechanism. As he punched it in on the pin pad on the side of the road, the gate roared to life and began to open.

The gate was about ten feet tall with barbed wire at the top slanted at an angle to make it more difficult to crawl over the top. It had caution reflectors all over it to keep anyone from missing it and accidentally running into it, and it was only able to be opened from the inside or by the pin pad on the outside. As the gate was opening, Jay hurried everyone in. "Hurry up and get in; that way we can close it right away and no other zombies will get in." He ran past them and looked around with his gun out just in case. His fingers were frozen but he'd break them off trying to pull that trigger if he had to. He ran into the guard booth, and each one of us in the group followed single file behind him. "I wanna shut that gate before it gets too far open," Jay said to particularly no one as he hit the gate close button on the side wall of the guard booth.

"Oh, my God, I never thought I'd be so happy to be warm. I love the snow, but this is not how I want my life to end; as a frozen Popsicle," Josh said.

"I agree with that. So now what?" Carron asked.

"Well, I'm thinking we should take a look around and see what's going on at the facility first before we go charging in. I wonder, should we put the padlock back on the gate?" Jay asked looking at Mark.

"I'm thinking that we should leave it off because if we have to run back out for any reason, we don't want to stop to fumble with the lock," Mark answered without looking up as he was rubbing Nikki's feet, trying to warm them up by the register.

"Good idea." Looking at the monitors, Jay watched as some of the governmental employees wandered around the facility zombified. There were bodies lying everywhere. The hallways looked like a blood bath, but some of the secure areas still had a zombie or two locked inside them. "I'm not sure I like this. It looks like someone tried to shoot their way out which is good because there's a path all the way up to the secure hallway that we need to get to." Pointing at the screen while everyone gathered around, "But I don't know if these people are dead, or undead, or already shot in the head and down for good."

"Guess the only way we can figure that out is to go and look. We just have to be prepared so I would suggest everyone check your guns and ammo because we may just have to blast our way out of here," Mark warned.

"Oh, fun," Josh grumbled.

Carron interrupted, Josh complaining, "Don't you think the best thing to do would be to wait until daylight comes so we can see? It's pitch black out there, and with the snow coming down, I can't see anything."

WINTER OF THE HUNGRY

"That might be a good idea, but with the horde of zombies just on the other side of the fence, I don't want to give them a chance to break through the gate and get inside. Then we'll be stuck in this guard shack full of windows and screwed," Jay retorted.

"Good thinking," I agreed. "As much as I don't want to go out in this snow again, I want to get off this island more."

"Agreed; let's get going." Mark put on his backpack and headed to the door. "I can't see anything out there, so here's hoping the snow isn't making the zombies invisible."

"Maybe they all froze; I mean, they're cold already because they're dead, so what's keeping them from becoming zombisicles?" joked Josh.

"You probably aren't far from the truth," Jay said, as he finished strapping on his guns. "The temperature in a person is what keeps them warm but if that person has no warmth to start with the colder air will freeze them faster. We might have a better chance outside with this wind."

"However, it would put us at risk of freezing to death if we stay outside in the dropping temperatures too," warned Carron.

As we headed out the door, each of us looked around, guns drawn, and Nikki was walking on her own since getting warm. She stayed close to the group. We only saw one zombie and he wasn't moving very fast; in fact, it looked like the only thing moving was his eyes. He was standing next to a door that said FACILITATOR ROOM on it.

"That's the door we have to go in. It's the only room that connects directly to the secure hallway; otherwise we'd have to go all the way through the plant." Jay pointed to the door on the other side of the parking area to show where they'd have to go in at.

As we got closer, the zombie started moving a little more, but not fast enough to worry anyone, except Carron. She started to freak out a bit. "Do we have to get so close to it? Why doesn't someone shoot it?"

WINTER OF THE HUNGRY

"We ran out of bullets for the silencer. He's not moving very fast; we'll just go around him. If we shoot him, we'd attract whatever else is out here that we can't see," I said as I looked around, a little paranoid myself.

Jay pulled out his key card and swiped it, but the light didn't turn green. "Damn cold freezes the card readers all the time. Kept telling them to add an external door to keep the readers warm." Jay swiped again and still got a red light. As we all were waiting for a green light, nobody noticed a couple zombies sneaking up from between the Facilitator Room and the building next to it. We just assumed the noise was the frozen one that was next to us. Finally, after the 5th swipe and Jay breathing on the reader, the light finally turned green, but not before Carron screamed.

"Aargh! They ..." Carron attempted to speak but her neck was already being ripped out as the second zombie starting pulling a part of her bicep muscle off and chewing it. She was already dead so the guys didn't have time to even draw their weapons to try and shoot her before she felt all the pain of having her flesh and muscles ripped to shreds. Nikki stood there barking at the zombies.

"Come on, it's too late for her; get inside!" Jay made sure they all got in and called for the dog, "Nikki! Come on girl!" Nikki barked a few more times and ran in behind Jay. Jay shut the door as the zombies dropped Carron and started moving towards it.

We were in a room that had maps of the plant and other papers thrown about, like someone had turned on a big fan in the room while a stack of papers had been sitting on the table. It seemed to be a conference type room, as there were no computers or any other kind of electronic devices, but just a table and a bunch of chairs.

"Okay, we got to keep moving." Grabbing one of the maps off the wall and pushing some papers over and off the table, Jay sat the map down. "This is where we are. We need to follow this

Winter of the Hungry

hallway down, which is the one that had all the hopefully dead bodies in it on the screens, and then key card into this hallway right here which leads straight out to the boat dock. If we get separated for any reason, if you come back down this hall and keep going you'll hit a door that has a button on the wall that slides it open by a pressure switch. This will lead you right into the facility. Once in, if you follow the outer wall on your left hand side all the way to the other side, you'll connect with this hallway here, which would lead you back to the secure hallway on the opposite side. It just goes in a giant circle. Everyone understand?"

We all agreed, and Mark led the our pack of survivors by opening the door to the hallway and checking to make sure that it was safe. No movement was visible in the hallway from any of the bodies that littered the floor. Slowly opening the door and stepping out into the hallway, we stepped over the bodies and didn't make a sound. The only sound was the clicking of Nikki's nails on the floor, so I picked her up and carried her, just in case.

WINTER OF THE HUNGRY

There was a red flashing light in the hallway which made it very difficult to focus on whether the bodies in the hallway were really moving or if it was just the flashing playing tricks on the eyes. When we came around the corner we saw that there were a few zombies wandering in the hallway between the secure door and the facility entrance. If we shot them, we'd risk waking up any that were still lying on the ground that just hadn't moved yet.

Looking at the group, Jay pointed to the zombies, held his finger to his lips, and pointed at the secure door and then to himself. Then we all nodded and Jay turned and started walking slowly up to the door and went to grab his key card. It slipped out of his hand and fell to the floor. Because that sound was the only sound in the hallway, the zombies heard it and others that were on the floor that weren't completely dead started to move. The ones already standing were quick, and Jay didn't have a chance to grab the key card and try again; he just turned and screamed, "Run!"

CHAPTER 14

WINTER OF THE HUNGRY

The four of us and Nikki, whom I had set down, ran down the hallway all the way to the other end jumping over the bodies both dead and moving. One caught Josh's leg, and in the struggle to get away he got scratched, but kept moving without saying a word to any of us. I got there first and hit the pressure switch button. As the door slid open, a few zombies started coming through from the facility side. I opened fire and started knocking them down to push my way through, Mark joined in next to me, and side by side we cleared a path into the facility. Jay and Nikki came through next and then Josh as Jay hit the pressure button to close the door behind him.

"Shit! How are we gonna get through to the secure hallway?" I asked as Mark and I turned around to look at the pile of zombie bodies we had made.

"Well, we can still go around the building and back in the other door. If the zombies followed us to this end, then hopefully there won't be any on that end. The corner is closer to that side so

WINTER OF THE HUNGRY

they shouldn't see us if we sneak in over there," Jay answered, catching his breath.

"We better get moving, though; I can hear others coming this way attracted by the gun shots," Mark said while re-loading his gun.

Jay led the way and walked around the left hand side of the facility with the group in tow. I looked around while we were walking making sure to keep an eye out for surprises. The red warning light was flashing in there also, so it made it more difficult to see into the corners and darker areas for danger. They walked down a walkway and around a corner; they could hear zombies moving around and groaning but didn't see any.

"Where are they at?" Josh asked quietly. "I can hear them but can't see them."

"There are seven floors in this facility. More than likely, the echo from the other floors is coming through the vents, and that's what we're hearing. Happens all the time on patrol; you could swear someone is standing next to you when they really may be two floors away," Jay answered as he kept moving.

We ducked under some piping and went around a corner where there was a door open to the outside. It was one of the side entrances to the center of the facility for government operators to do experiments outside. Snow was blowing in through the door, and Jay reached over and closed and latched it.

"Can we get to the secure hallway or the boat launch any faster going through there?" I wondered.

"No, that is just one giant circle also and only has a few access doors leading inside. I'd rather be inside dealing with the zombies than outside and find the other access doors blocked or something," Jay responded. "Let's keep moving."

We continued our way through the facility, walking around different machines that only had words and letters to state what they were. There was a giant silo shaped machine that said TQR15-12. "What's that?" asked Josh.

WINTER OF THE HUNGRY

"It's a pressure tester. You put anything you want on the inside and it starts either building pressure up or taking pressure out of the room to see how much the object can handle. The only reason I know is I saw it used once on an apple. You can see through the window around the corner." Jay pointed as they walked by.

What the group saw in the window, though, was not an apple. Apparently someone had hid in the room or was locked in the room and the machine was turned on. There was a bloody mess everywhere from the walls, to the floor, and even some on the ceiling.

"Talk about testing your blood pressure," snickered Josh.

I just groaned and punched him in the arm.

"What? It was funny!"

They continued on to the opposite wall. "We're gonna turn right here and head back towards the other door," Jay explained, pointing ahead of him at the door which they could barely see through the red flashing lights.

The zombie noises and groans kept getting louder, but Josh still couldn't see where they were coming from. "I don't like this. I'm grateful and all, but we should have seen at least one zombie or something, shouldn't we?"

"Well, if everyone evacuated when the emergency lights went on, then probably not. Most people are either on the other floors or in secure areas where they won't be wandering around in the hallways." But Jay was getting nervous too, he knew that the louder those sounds got, the less likely they were echoes through a vent.

There was a relay room just to the right between us and the hallway door we needed to get to. The relay room door was always shut and secured because it contained several interconnected supercomputers, so to speak, that allowed the employees to integrate certain plug-and-play connectivity. They assisted with the main facility's power supply and boosted the heating, lighting, air-conditioning and other electrical conditions for the millions of tests that were done on site at any given time. These machines kept all other machines from shutting down due to overloading. The only reason this was so significant was there would be, on a normal day, anywhere from 30-50 employees in this room, and as Jay got closer, he noticed the door was open.

Jay stopped in his tracks and help up a hand, and turned back to look at the group. In a whisper he explained, "The only way that door could be closed is from the inside. It's an automatic door that was built into the system and a certain code has to typed in on the keyboard that is just inside the door. The door won't budge if you try to push it or pull it. There is always someone in that room because it's a cyber secured area and is never left unattended, so there is always someone to open the door." Jay also explained how many people are usually in there, and why they kept hearing the noises getting louder the whole time they were in there.

"So, how do we get past the door without being seen?"

Mark asked. "I'm assuming we can't just send someone in there to close the door?"

"No, the door closes on a spring so once the code is typed in, you have about five seconds before the door slams shut. There isn't enough time to get from the keyboard to the door before that time. Maybe we can go up a floor or two and come down on the other side and then take ..."

"What's the code?" interrupted Josh.

"What? Why? You got a death wish?" I sneered at Josh.

Lifting up his pant leg, Josh showed the group the scratch.

"No," I gasped. "When?"

"When we were in the hallway. That one that grabbed my leg. I didn't wanna say anything, figured I could continue to help until it was getting close. Now here's my chance."

"But there might be a cure, right?" I didn't want to lose my best friend. "You're the last person I have left in my life, dude." Sniffing just a little, I hugged Josh.

WINTER OF THE HUNGRY

While Mark and Jay kept a look out, Josh and I had a heart to heart. "Listen, Itch, you were the one person I met when I came here that wanted to be my friend. You made me feel welcome even when there were so many more that didn't. I wouldn't have survived this long on this island without your friendship and I appreciate that. You saved me, now let me save you." Turning and looking at Jay, he asked, "What's the code?"

"4-2-8-B-F-X-9"

"Here's my ammo, but I'm keeping the gun and one bullet. After I lock the door ..."

"Don't you dare say it!" Cutting Josh off, I didn't want to hear the end of that sentence. "You were like the brother I never had, Josh."

"Ditto." Josh walked over to the door and peered slowly around the corner. The whole room was a circle and there was one window on the other side of the door where, if they would have just walked by, the zombies would have seen them and they would have been done for. Josh looked back at his best friend and took a deep breath. He'd been resaying the code over and over in his head so he didn't forget it. "4-2-8-B-F-X-9 ... 4-2-8-B-F-X-9 ... 4-2-8-B-F-X-9 ... here goes nothing." Josh ran into the room grabbed the keyboard and typed the code in as he said it out loud to himself, "4-2-8-B-F-X-9." The door came crashing down and the 30+ zombies in the room came at him.

Mark, Jay, and I walked by the door just as it closed and we saw this brave individual looking back at us. Mark and Jay continued walking, pulling me along, not wanting me to witness what was about to happen. As we got to the door we heard, "You zombie scum, EAT ME!" And then the gun went off.

I was very sad, but had to chuckle as my friend always knew how to make a situation funny. I would never forget him.

Jay looked through the security door and saw that some of the zombies had wandered back down the hall but not many and it was still possible to get to the secure hallway without calling too much attention to ourselves. "Only use your knives, guys. We can't make too much noise if we want to get out of here."

Mark and I grabbed our knives and stood at the ready. Nodding at each other, Jay opened the door, and the three dashed in and started stabbing the four zombies that were at this end. Having only one arm, Mark was having a little more trouble with his knife and got it stuck in one of their heads. "Shit!"

The commotion from the attack alerted the other zombies in the hall as Jay finally got the green light on the door and he and I and Nikki dashed through. "Just leave it!" yelled Jay, but as Mark let go, another zombie bumped the door before he could make it through and it secured shut. Mark started shooting but ran out of ammo.

"This is just a fine how do you do." Mark was gonna go back around, but the gunshot from Josh had attracted zombies on the other side of the door and now Mark was stuck. Jay couldn't reopen the door because there were too many zombies around and not enough bullets. Mark pulled a grenade out of his knapsack as the zombies closed in and seeing Jay through the door, they just acknowledged that it was the only way.

"Run, Itchy; now!" Jay and I took off down the secure hallway and were trying to get to the other end before the grenade went off. Jay was fumbling with the key card and just got the door open when there was an explosion. Jay and I flew through the door onto the snow. Little explosions started happening throughout the facility due to some of the chemicals and other matter they were testing there. Rolling over, "We've got to get to the boats; this place is going to go sky high in a minute!" Jay jumped up and pulled me to my feet and we ran to the boats.

"Wait! Where's Nikki? Nikki? Come here girl!" I yelled for her, and saw her lying in the snow. I ran over and grabbed her; she was just shaken up a bit but all right. We ran to the boats and got on board. While I was tending to Nikki looking for any cuts or breaks, Jay started the boat.

WINTER OF THE HUNGRY

The commotion attracted a zombie that had been on board down below and he had started up the stairs towards me. Jay saw him come up and dove at him before there was even a sound to be made. They dove into the water and being as cold as it was the zombie had no warmth to keep it from instantly freezing. However in the attack, Jay had gotten bit in the shoulder. He climbed back into the boat and sat down. "Looks like this is the end of the road for me Itchy."

"No, seriously?" I looked at the bite. "This can't be happening. I can't be the only survivor."

"Looks like it, man. Tell the story, hey? Tell people what happened here. Don't let the government cover it up. Make people listen so this doesn't happen again elsewhere, okay?"

"Okay, I promise."

"I'm gonna go below deck and make sure that everything is safe. I can't go with you. The risk of this getting off the island is just too great. I don't want other people in the world in danger

WINTER OF THE HUNGRY

because I was too chicken to do what was necessary."

Jay walked below and I just sat watching the little explosions here and there throughout the facility while the boat bobbed in the water. I couldn't help thinking that it made no sense to get all that way and then be the only person left.

Jay came up from below, "You and Nikki should go below. You can steer from down there and keep warm. Head straight to the mainland."

"What about you?"

"I'm gonna go back on the island and take care of what needs to be taken care of. It was very nice meeting you, Itchy." Taking my hand, he said, "You are a very brave young man." Jay let go of my hand and got back on the dock.

I watched as Jay took all the last of the grenades and ammo and set it all next to a building labeled with the sign COMBUSTIBLE CHAMBER.

"Now get out of here!" Jay yelled back at me.

WINTER OF THE HUNGRY

I revved the engine and pushed forward through the water, heading away from the dock. I turned and looked back and knew what Jay was doing. I saw him pull the pin on the grenade and look back at me one last time. Seven seconds later there was a giant explosion that detonated the rest of the materials in the bag and then the chamber itself. I ducked as the chamber when up and there was a giant synchronized booming of buildings as each one went up.

I looked back at what used to be my island home. All he could see now as I got farther away from the island was fire, and all I felt was sorrow, pain, and sadness with what used to be a happy place with so many awesome memories. Now it would just be the place of nightmares.

A couple hours later ...

"Pull him out of there!" yelled an armed guard with the military. They pulled Nikki and I off the boat. "Are you all right, son? Medic!"

WINTER OF THE HUNGRY

A medic rushed over and covered me with a blanket and led me over to the ambulance. While the medic was checking him out, a newspaper reporter rushed over to get the scoop of her lifetime with the only known survivor of the horrible accident on the little island Marksburg.

. . . .

"And that's what happened." I told the reporter.

"That's an amazing story. You have lost so much."

I ... I don't feel so well," I said as I laid down in the back of the ambulance. The medic started checking vitals and then I stopped breathing. One of the other EMT's closed the back of the ambulance door.

"Keep filming," the reporter told her cameraman. "That was an unbelievable story from a scared and exhausted young man who is still fighting for his life ..."

All of a sudden there were screams from the back of the ambulance and back doors swung open and out jumped one of the

WINTER OF THE HUNGRY

EMT's holding his neck, screaming, "He bit me!" The EMT dashed from the ambulance and into the crowd.

Right behind him was Itchy. The reporter gasped, realizing the story that had just been told was true, and Itchy, somewhere in his fight for survival, had gotten scratched and turned after he thought himself to be safe. He jumped out and ran straight at the camera. The last thing the cameraman saw was Itchy's face filling up the lens.

EPILOGUE

WINTER OF THE HUNGRY

Sunrise came and as the bright light started to show up on the snow covered ground, the flashing lights of the ambulances and police squad cars disappeared in the radiant glow. There were a few bodies lying about the ground and some smoke coming from a car that had hit a tree, but other than that there was stillness about the boat dock. Miles down the road there was movement; you could see a young lady, missing a shoe, slowly limping down the road. She had blood dripping down her left arm and a microphone in the other with the torn wire dragging behind her.

She stopped only for a second because she had heard something but the sound disappeared and she continued on her way to find something or someone to eat.

The sound had come from the snow covered bushes alongside the road where a lonely dog hid within, whimpering and waiting for someone to save her ...

ABOUT THE AUTHOR

Tiffany Kleiman was born and raised in Michigan and continues to live there with her husband, her son, their 3 cats, and their dog.

She's currently working on her Master's Degree in Criminal Justice with a concentration in Cybercrime and Cyber Security. After she graduates she hopes to continue on to receive her Doctorate.

She enjoys writing, spending time outdoors, and being with family in her spare time.

WINTER OF THE HUNGRY

PREVIOUS PUBLICATIONS

Only a Dream 1999 printed in *Serendipity* - a collection of student writings from Bay de Noc Community College

A Little Time 2000 printed in *Serendipity* - a collection of student writings from Bay de Noc Community College

The Secret Door 2003 printed in *Theatre Of The Mind* by Noble House Publishers-London, Paris, and New York

Goodbye 2004 printed in *The Best Poems and Poets Of 2003* by the International Library of Poetry - Maryland

A Little Time c. 2005 reprinted in *The Layers of Our Lives* by the International Library of Poetry - Maryland

My love for you (how big is it?) 2012 printed in *International Who's Who in Poetry* by the International Who's Who in Poetry - California

The Haunting at Thorton Mansion 2014 printed by CreateSpace – South Carolina

81242485R00146

Made in the USA
Columbia, SC
27 November 2017